A PERFECT STILLNESS

CONVERSATIONS FROM THE UNCONSCIOUS

A PERFECT STILLNESS

CONVERSATIONS FROM THE UNCONSCIOUS

Short Fiction by
J.L. COOPER

Carmichael, CA / 2018

Introduction

It's a unique challenge to write fictional accounts of psychotherapy when the author is also a practicing psychologist. Our everyday encounters take place in more contexts than we are aware of, calling for images and descriptions that never conform to a simple appreciation of me, you, ours, distilling and hiding explanations, illuminating wish and need.

These are not disguised stories about actual persons in therapy; they are stories of imagined people, often collective tributes representing all the therapy with women who have been violated, also men in search of meaning, love, culture and family, or finding meaning in relationships when the past has led to pain. A story emerges in a language of intimate construction. Some of these tales are not concerned with therapy; the connecting theme is always the richness of subjective life and our influence on each other's deepest regions, which can occur within the first moments of meeting.

Acknowledgments

I'm grateful to the editors and judges of the following publications and where these works were first published.

A Son in Tennessee
District Lit, November, 2017
Finalist in 2017 District Lit Flash Fiction Contest

High Noon with Pink Carnations
Tic-Toc an Anthology, Kind of A Hurricane Press, 2014

Path of the Ground Birds
Winner of *Tupelo Quarterly Prose Open Prize*, TQ9, 2016
Judged by Pulitzer Prize winner Adam Johnson

The Couple that May Still Live on Maple Street
Structo, UK, 2016

When Moon and Sun Were Close
The Sonder Review, 2016

Table of Contents

A Streak of Red on Gray

Forget reason; nothing is reasonable. Still, there has to be a start. Normally, when offering therapy to a couple, Dr. Waverly tells the two it will be different than individual therapy since he focuses on tensions between parties, their impasses and collusions, the clash of histories, their unexplored languages. But the seasoned Manhattan psychologist never delivered his introduction to the well-dressed couple in front of him. His dream from the night before haunted him and gave him mighty pause. In the dream he was standing in their living room, unseen, but retained a keen awareness that he would soon meet them in the usual way—the following day in fact. He had no time to consult a colleague, much less a mystic, before the couple opened the thick walnut door to his waiting room. Ernst Waverly pretended not to be shaken, but of course he was, and found himself offering an extra measure of reserve when he extended seating choices of couch and chair.

He was unnerved when the woman abruptly fixed herself in the chair closest to the door, exactly like the woman in his dream. Likewise, her husband behaved as the gentleman in the dream, frowning in capitulation while camping out in the middle of

Waverly's full-size couch. The image of the two, with discontent etched on their faces, reminded Waverly of an actual painting he saw in a modern art museum.

The portrait was an abstract of a man and woman seated, not looking at each other. With a twinge in his spine, he realized the same portrait appeared on a wall in his dream, in the living room, where streaks of red made frequent appearances in art and vases. Smaller objects filled the spaces: little statues, busts of sculpted heads, spiral shells and a tuning fork. Objects filled every shelf in the room. To top it off, a small bust resembling Waverly's deceased wife rested among the treasures.

It's a good thing Waverly had a treasure of his own; a small hand-painted frog carved from pine was looking down from a high shelf in the bookcase, nestled among hundreds of books on psychotherapy. Waverly had always wondered if the frog makes himself invisible, since not one patient had commented on his presence in his entire thirty-five year career.

The frog appeared to him at a craft fair the same week Waverly received his license to practice. The most compelling feature was a conservative green tie carved into the chest, as if to signify he's a working frog, not a garden decoration. Waverly didn't hesitate to claim his new office companion, using the simple name Frog, since he didn't want to get carried away with a fanciful notion. But it was too late. He was already carried away, and since that day it's never been clear to Waverly if it was a wishful thought or a thoughtful wish that he animate the frog, but either way, he assigned Frog the impossible role of watcher, whom he vowed to consult freely.

What the hell was that about? he asked Frog, after particularly confusing therapy sessions. He never talked to Frog in front of humans; imagine how it might look. Although he consulted several fine colleagues on his psychotherapy cases, Frog was always present in the real encounters, and held him to a private standard.

Let it be known, Frog never spoke, not once, but that never stopped Waverly from an imagined conversation. His habit was to bring his open hand to his forehead, glance around the room for an afterimage of his patient, then release his hand to travel down the continent of his long serious face, making stops along the way, like a night train stopping at the edge of skin and beard, pausing again at the lips, until he found the curve of his chin.

He listened for the whisper of a muse, as if Frog had asked; *you saw the omission, didn't you,* (or) *what do you hope I know?* Waverly never regretted his fantasy that Frog had the ability to hear everything, know his mind, even make small interventions, like stopping time when necessary. That talent was desperately needed yesterday, when Waverly was riveted to a lucid, seventy-five minute session with his new couple.

<h3 style="text-align:center">OPENINGS</h3>

The couple offered themselves as Natalie Chase and Spencer Mason, married for seven years, parents to a three-year-old daughter, Bryce. They had successful early careers, teaching math in different colleges. Neither would say it, but the regions around their eyes told Waverly that life was beginning to grind against their hopes. Both were miserable but neither wanted a divorce.

Spencer began speaking before Waverly had a chance to settle into his dark leather chair. It was less than a minute into the session, but Waverly couldn't help surmising the structure of their connection. It's an occupational hazard to think you're onto something. Hypotheses float in the air like ashes after a forest fire.

There's no need to single one out as evidence of the fire. Still, Spencer's urgency to be first to speak seemed a kind of payback to his wife for her presumption to grab the chair he would have otherwise taken. One never knows the real start of a session, probably in childhood fantasies of the therapist. Waverly wanted to be Green Lantern at seven, using his power ring to stop an asteroid from destroying the earth. Nothing less than that seemed interesting. It didn't occur to him to use the ring to save his parents' marriage.

In therapy, even the occasional sense of certainty can be an illusion. It's like going fishing with a friend. You both see the pole bending, but the prize gets away before you can pull it to shore. There you go, insisting it was a gigantic bass or catfish. The friend smiles, saying he's snagged numerous beer cans and bicycle tires that behaved exactly that way in the current. Waverly always thought an impasse is not really an impasse if it leads to a discussion of what is imagined.

Spencer recounted the fight that brought the pair in for consultation. Civility was breached, taking on the quality of a marathon. They went at it until 2:00 A.M. in a toe-to-toe tirade that started in the kitchen and ended in the laundry room with wet clothes all over the floor.

Waverly listened carefully to Spencer's introduction, but reserved a portion of his thoughts for his first observation, that Spencer wasn't quick enough to grab the chair he wanted. Spencer presented himself as a reasonable man in a dead-end canyon, as if he thought his wife would not give an accurate summary of their circumstances. In any case, he didn't want her to interfere with his opening.

In parts not said, in nuances and minor pauses, Waverly kept thinking of the way Spencer settled himself in the middle of the couch, offering his best frown. He wouldn't be relying on the anchors represented by end tables, or notice the presence of tissues on one of them. Sometimes, people simply have a cold, and reach for comfort there. Not everything is grief and tears.

There was something more. Spencer didn't seem to notice anything in the room, whereas Natalie immediately took a virtual walk in the office with her eyes. He didn't notice the Japanese lamp, the collection of vases, or the literature on the shelf next to the couch. If a person browsed the titles, they'd be ushered into the world of characters. Spencer seemed to regard them as props, whereas his wife squinted to make out the titles.

Once Waverly accepted Spencer's need to speak first, he released himself to appreciate that Natalie made herself a veiled figure. He noticed the path of her eyes. She was a listener and a watcher, but not of her husband. She might even have suspected Frog's presence in the bookshelf and kept it to herself. Observations were suspended in Waverly's mind, like tadpoles swimming in the shallows of a pond, not ready for metamorphosis.

As Spencer talked, Waverly experienced a tremor of recognition, a breeze from an open door. There was something vital about Spencer's mind—not because of similarities to his own marriage, which ended the year before with the loss of his wife to cancer— but from a sense that Spencer, like himself, secured himself to a memory, then revised its importance in favor of an emerging thought, like he was discovering a larger intention mid-sentence. Waverly had been doing that all his life.

There was more. The expressions on Spencer's face changed frequently, sensitively, as if different objects kept showing up in his hand, but when he looked, he had no recollection of having reached for them. His peculiar way of catching up to the here-and-now was kindred to Waverly's style. Frog is narrating this part, since Waverly is preoccupied.

Spencer continued, as if summarizing a case in front of a court. His voice was beautifully resonant, full of eloquence, using long sentences filled with airbrush strokes of self-reflection. He shifted to minor keys, some illuminated or slightly haunted, in which entire stories were suspected between commas. The effect on Waverly was hypnotic.

Although Waverly didn't ask for any history, Spencer explained how Natalie won his affection when she was a student in his calculus class. She returned his goofy smile with a wordless qualification, as if she had said, *look my way and I'll lock on your gaze, plus I'll add something that makes you keep looking. You'll be forbidden to know what it is, but it's plenty good!*

Spencer's marriage proposal to Natalie came to his mind the day they met; a perfect version of one plus one. It was his first job out of graduate school. She was a first year graduate student, with a curious mix of confidence and obscurity. Spencer recounted that Natalie summoned a sequence of expressions over a matter of seconds, using only her eyes, which communicated she was (a) interested, (b) amused, and (c) hopeful, outlined just for him.

When Natalie confirmed this sequence on their first date and praised him for deciphering it, everything was roses and mirrors. *End of search,* he mused, just under his breath. He took Natalie's hand from across the dining table and told her that his breath could not be measured when he spotted her for the first time in class. He recalled her exact response and delivered it to Waverly.

"Actually these things can be measured if measurement is your goal. Your blood pressure, pulse rate, volume of breath, galvanic skin resistance, and even subtle eye movements can be measured. Is there something else you're trying to say?"

Her smile pointed to the fact she loved drawing him off-center, delicately, playfully, clearly in her direction. Spencer relished the unpredictability of being attracted to her. She used her eyes with tenacity when it suited her, evoking images never taught in math. On that same first date, she began nibbling, carefully, on a piece of bread, which she knew would drive him crazy. She might as well have been kissing his ear. He saw she was giving him permission to trace her curves, first with his eyes, then his hands, his real hands, later that night.

He told Waverly he wanted that version of Natalie back, and couldn't stand the thought that courtship might have been the best part of their life together. He glanced at Natalie, telling of his wish to be the piece of bread again, but she was taking a walk among dabs of red in Waverly's office portrait of an autumn path. It was an abstract of fallen leaves on a dirt path in a forest. She left behind a slight pale smile.

In the same instant, Waverly found himself drifting to the memory of his first date with his own wife, Cynthia, who was with him for twenty-seven years. Frog noted that Waverly and Natalie could see each other, but only within the portrait. Natalie was walking nearby and he leaned against a tree. Frog needed to freeze the therapy session to allow Waverly his reflection.

Cynthia McBride gave young Dr. Waverly a hint of bedroom eyes; the same summoning brown eyes he easily finds in her photos. Eyes don't seem to age with the rest of the body—a fact insufficiently studied by psychiatry—but well known among lovers and authors. When he dropped her off at her apartment after their first date, after a dud of a movie, both agreed their conversation was far more interesting than any movie ever made.

It was winter. Each breath quickly vanished on the doorstep of her apartment. She allowed a kiss on the lips, and pressed her hand behind his neck to pull him in for more. Waverly, who was economical with words, replied, "I would love a lifetime of this." As it turned out, he had such a lifetime, was grateful for a hundred qualities in Cynthia, and cursed by only a few. They worked through rough spots with separate vacations and wonderful friends. Their fights were merely occasional—the kind that lovers have—where the goal of repair was equal to the need to win a point. The impoverished themes were put to bed under thick woolen blankets. Occasionally, one of them slept in the guest bedroom and never spoke of it. They were childless by agreement, content with dogs and a rooftop garden, and loved to see what kinds of whales live in every portion of the globe.

Cynthia was an artist, working in oil when she became ill; she'd been experimenting with thin streaks of red against delicate patterns of gray that were often mixed with blue. Always, she was trying new angles of approach, which evoked a muse-like, erotic distraction in Waverly, taking him away from the parts of him that wanted solutions. Frog knows well how Cynthia's images play in him, especially the reds on the horizon at sunset and the edges of storm clouds in the tropics.

When she lost her energy, she'd been exploring this new arena, unsatisfied with recent renderings. Cynthia didn't say much about the image she was working on when she went to the hospital for the last time. Waverly wondered if it represented some kind of cancellation, an angry bit, a line splitting the universe into self and other, the known from the unknowable, or herself from this world. When he asked about the red line, she paused and looked at it with curiosity, as if it only appeared when she wasn't looking. Then he realized his folly; to ask for an explanation requires words imposed on a symphony of meanings. But she had a response this time, this one time.

"It's an invitation I make for myself. Feel free to get lost. This one wants to be wild. It could possibly be my most honest painting."

Nothing more was said. Neither Waverly nor the best doctors could stop the illness. She's with the cattail reeds now, rustling his mind with the slightest breeze.

Frog felt the weight of moment, and mercifully suspended the session a little longer, freezing everyone in their poses to allow Waverly to collect himself. Fortunately, Waverly lived in the certainty of having loved, but had not been able to reconcile himself to the emptiness of a bitter page that rejected his words every time he tried to write about Cynthia. He ended up planting fourteen dahlias in the yard of their summer home in Vermont; each represented a line of a sonnet he couldn't write. He couldn't describe her saucer eyes with justice, and took to wondering; on what Oregon beach, with fourteen monumental rocks offshore, would his memories fix themselves and reside?

Her final abstract portrait remains where she left it, in her studio in their home, on the eighteenth floor on the Upper West Side, covered by an off-white cloth. It was the first October since she passed. Now, with the couple in his office, he felt the kick of an amphibian leg in his ribs, which was Frog's way of resuming time. Now in the present, Waverly realized he was unprepared for the first red leaves of October. He saw them calling as he walked across Central Park on his old familiar path. It's just that he wasn't ready for them to be red. It was the same way he noticed something stirring in Natalie. He turned his swivel chair to face her directly, since she seemed to be reaching for an opening remark.

The second Natalie noticed Waverly being curious about her, she crossed her legs and leaned a few inches forward. It was amazing how she'd been listening all along. She stepped out of the office portrait, into the session, then turned back and ran to a different area of the painting. This time Waverly found her between the trees and off the path, deep in the abstract leaves. Only twenty seconds had gone by, but they were the longest twenty seconds in Waverly's career because he sensed the woman in his dream needed to be wild. Not coy, just wild. Frog saw this part clearly; Cynthia's explorations found new life in Natalie Chase. Naturally, Waverly had to follow.

Spencer didn't seem to notice what was happening between Natalie and Waverly, and continued talking about their first date. He came to the part where Natalie proclaimed him to be the last to appreciate his own natural charm. He wanted to believe it, but conceded that once he believed it, there was no going back. He was drunk in it. Now, in marriage, he was guilty of becoming demanding, for no good cause, boring in tiny ways, expecting her to find him charming even when he wasn't. Spencer admitted he'd been unfair, a confession he hoped she would resonate with, even sympathize with, but Natalie was still in the forest.

Waverly had a thought of his own just then. *Therapy cannot be so tidy. What if I'm still stuck in my dream of this couple, the one I had before meeting them?* Frog refused to suspend time, not wanting to make it a habit. Humans get lazy if you do. Waverly had to remind himself that it's possible to cultivate self-awareness within dreams, but either way, he appreciated Spencer's apology, setting a tone far removed from the dreary blame-fest in couple's therapy. Natalie didn't budge, and had the odd confidence of a poker player sitting on a flush, acting like she might draw a card anyway, as if she was unsure, when really she wasn't.

Spencer held fast the stage, saying his own mother looked after him, but that was his best and only description. Waverly knew to hold off any questions just then. Suddenly there were too many voices in the room. Spencer's mother was trying to yell something at Frog, while Spencer's father, who wasn't mentioned, rode in and out of the room on a unicycle. Waverly wanted to see where momentum would build, and kept an eye on Natalie. When she didn't blink, Spencer chose the moment to speak of an equal sign that appeared in his mind when he first met Natalie. It had a word on either side of it: *compelling* and *shattering*. His self-analysis stopped there. Perhaps Waverly could help. He added that he couldn't locate Natalie when she distanced herself from him. Frog thought, *like right now?*

Nobody spoke for another thirty-five seconds. *Ah,* thought Waverly, *the first actual complaint: a foothold.* He realized Spencer didn't speculate that his comment could have easily been stated in reverse, that he couldn't locate himself in the moments of his wife's withdrawal, and it set off a little panic. Attentive frogs know the problem well. They know the feeling is frightening, like jumping into an abyss on a moonless night, hoping for a pond. You wish for the safety of water, to hide in stillness near the base of reeds, knowing that motion gives you away. But perhaps there's no water at all. Sometimes an abyss is just an abyss.

This last thought leapt off the page at Waverly; the way a frog jumps twenty times it's length. He wondered what the woman in his dream would have to say, since Natalie, until now, said nothing. To his astonishment, the voice from the woman in his dream readily whispered to him from the bookshelf.

"My dear Dr. Waverly, why don't you ask Spencer why he doesn't want sex with me anymore?"

As for Waverly, no ghost from his dream would have guessed these realms. He wasn't about to be bossed around by a character from a stupid dream, but in his dream he was numb, unable to muster a thought while standing in the living room of the couple. He wondered what his own therapist would say; perhaps he entered a scene he witnessed with his own parents, triggered by the first time he heard Spencer's ultra-reasonable voice.

Coldness descended in the consulting room the second Spencer ended his soliloquy, saying he had the sad assumption Natalie didn't love him anymore. Then, with the timing of a Shakespearian actor, he turned toward her to complete his apology.

"I'm sorry for the things I said during our fruitless argument the other night."

But his voice drifted to a quality of being a little too much in love with his sincerity, as if the marriage would now begin to heal. He went back to describe the first time he called upon her in class, when he rose from his soft pine chair, sensing hints of her desire. In Waverly's dream, a similar pine chair was in their living room, but it was empty.

COMPLICATIONS

Shit, thought Waverly, *I'm in some deep trouble here. Whose dream am I in?* Natalie had a way of listening with arms and legs firmly crossed. The way she held her arms across her chest seemed important, not lost on Waverly, who also saw she had uncanny auburn eyes, deeply hidden, resting uncomfortably between high cheeks in tension with slightly uneven bangs the color of cottonwood bark. She was keenly aware of him visiting her space. In the dream she was less stunning, sadder, and was fuming about something. This version of Natalie was patient, controlled, waiting for a moment of her choosing.

Finally, carefully, she began to speak, as if addressing the air between men everywhere. She spoke of an erosion of affection and basic consideration since their daughter was born, and wondered if Spencer was having an affair. This brought a rise from him.

"What the hell? It's you I need and love. I don't want another woman. Is that really what you think?"

She dropped that hot potato, then, as if to one-up her husband in lyricism, she turned toward Waverly to offer her own version of their how they first met, in a sea of quirks and graphs in class.

"Spencer has it basically accurate. I played along, pretending to be interested in the analysis of data sitting just a few inches from my eyes. We had a mutual love of graphs and numbers, trends and anomalies, dips and spikes on paper. He made no secret of liking my long skirts, even though I'm not so tall or classically shaped. I didn't like my body at all, but he thought I had killer legs, and that was enough for me. I remember his double take the day I wore a blouse patterned like fine graph paper, matched with a plain black skirt, just to drive him crazy. I wanted his hands all over me. But there was another truth. I didn't know what to do with such power." Then she detached, right in the middle of her story. The effect was equivalent to interrupting a Chopin etude to get a glass of water. When she had the men leaning in for more, she resumed.

"A blank sheet of graph paper begs for reference points, to be drawn upon slowly, carefully, deliberately, don't you think, Dr. Waverly?"

At that moment, Waverly imagined the seriousness of her sensuality, and hoped Spencer would appreciate what she was saying. But Spencer interrupted, wrecking Natalie's moment. It was horribly timed, a felony of the marital kind.

"Don't fall for it, Dr. Waverly, she's doing it again. From day one she's tortured me with anticipation. She still does. From the instant I saw her, I wanted to touch her shoulder and work my way down to her legs, but the only excuse I could think of was that of a fifteen year old boy dropping a pencil, suddenly catching myself on her leg, feigning apology. That's how mesmerized I was. I actually wondered if it was her fantasy too, sent to me telepathically."

"Please, let me finish," insisted Natalie. "I've been wondering, Dr. Waverly, if I still have any appeal to him at all."

She spoke like her husband wasn't even in the room. "I don't like what's happened to my body since having a child. It's true; I used to love driving him crazy. I don't even think of that anymore. He won't notice."

Spencer covered his entire face with his hands, making himself small. *Ah*, thought Waverly, *a Roman wall. I'll come back to this, or more to the point, it will come back to us, like a tide that always returns.*

To her credit, Natalie did not crush her husband further just then, although she easily could have. Instead, she admitted that Spencer had a unique way of appreciating the whole of her, but never all at once.

"When we're getting along, it feels very nice, the way a summer breeze asks for hints of spice."

My God she's incredible, thought Waverly. But he imagined her in childhood as a person so logical that nobody ever though to offer her a nickname. She must have read his mind, because she announced that Spencer had a nickname from the time he was ten years old—it was Sparky.

"Where's your spark, Mr. Sparky?" she asked her husband.

From his perch in the bookshelf, Frog, who is omnipotent, and slightly maddening for this quality, perked up right away. Waverly sensed a sea change too. Natalie had introduced a Trojan horse into the session by the nickname business, making everything more surreal.

Spencer volunteered, defensively, he was proud of his nickname, which became attached to him like a second birth when he was only ten. He had learned to imitate the bark of a friend's dog, which gained neighborhood fame by going crazy at barbeques when coals were lit with lighting fluid. The dog would bark ferociously at the fire, and some people laughed at the terrified dog. Frog has never been able to understand the cruelty of humans.

Spencer was the exception; the only one who comforted the dog with touch. When Spencer held him firmly, the dog stopped being terrified, and went around begging for food, expecting treats as if he was responsible for putting the fire out. Frog offered into Waverly's mind that the dog's perspective might be a clue as to how to help the couple. From his wooden presence, Frog observed that the dog must have experienced a sequence of fear, followed by a soothing touch, with no conflicted awareness, no human-like confusion or ambivalence or need to understand a damn thing. The scene always ended with the dog being his old endearing self. That's all Spencer remembered about his nickname, so of course he wanted to inhabit it again as if it would help him get his mojo back; he wanted a little praise and soothing from his wife. Trouble was, as Frog observed, Natalie didn't speak that language.

Waverly, under advisement from Frog, asked, "Do you recall who gave you the nickname?"

Spencer lifted his eyes to the ceiling and reported a fresh memory of a sweet girl in attendance, a relative of a neighbor. He remembered she wore a skirt, and had just come from a piano recital. Her name was Lucien. She alone observed that Spencer's kindness to the dog was meritorious, and should spark others to acknowledge his actions.

"I name you Sparky," she said, pointing in a regal manner at Spencer (not the dog, who already had a name). She was only seven, but her comment sustained him for over two decades. He always liked the fit of the name, and others came to use it with affection.

"My God, how could I have forgotten that nice girl?" he said. "All the images come back: the skirt, the sparks, the sweet dog, the soothing touches, Lucien's playfulness—all of it forms a bridge to you, sweet Natalie."

Once he uttered this (as if it were a math solution infused with a psychoanalytic twist), Spencer Mason was doomed. Natalie was doomed too, because she'd made fun of the nickname more than a few times, calling him, well, the opposite of what sparks do. But she'd never heard the Lucien part. All he said to his wife was, "Don't fuck with my nickname ever again." He turned to glare at the wall.

Whether displaced or misplaced, embellished or obscured, Natalie said the nickname business flares up (grinning at her own Freudian slip) whenever the couple has major tension. She said *SORRY* to Spencer, sheepishly, and admitted she's never examined whether she's jealous or envious, since she has no nickname herself. In any case, she wanted him to appreciate that she didn't give her man his nickname, and didn't want to use it automatically.

"Lovers are supposed to invent their own language," she observed. Waverly thought of a hot iron that burns long after you turn it off.

Thirty Minutes In

Everyone took a breather and had a sip of something. Waverly took a swig of cold coffee, Natalie softened her lips with Irish Breakfast tea, and Spencer gulped his bottled water. Natalie announced it was time they got around to telling Dr. Waverly about their argument. She wanted to tell this part, and put her hand up like a stop sign to Spencer, who wanted to be first to tell this part.

"Not now, math-boy," she said, in an oddly appealing way. "Bryce, our three-year-old, asked us a simple question: 'Mommy, Daddy, where is this line going?' and pointed to a drawing that went off the edge of the paper, onto the kitchen table, down the table leg, up and over the chair, across the floor, then up the wall in red crayon, as far as her arm would reach. She expected praise, but I was appalled."

Waverly was thinking about the sweet child's point of view, imagining Bryce in a Norman Rockwell image. Frog sent out a warning. Spencer rushed the stage in anger.

"Tell him. Tell him what you did! You punished Bryce, right when I was going to give her ten feet of cardboard in the garage to draw on as she pleased. I was going to tell her we don't draw on the tables and walls, ever. At most a brief time out. I was upset too, but it didn't occur to me to scream at her like Natalie did. Dr. Waverly, can you believe Natalie punished her by making her scrub everything down with soapy water. She yanked Bryce to her room and shut out the light. I couldn't believe it. Our daughter does not have serious behavior problems. She was crying the whole time, ashamed and confused. She still doesn't know what she did wrong. She's just over three years old."

It was Waverly's turn to put up a caution sign, as if it read *mountain curves ahead*. He cautioned Spencer, saying he just interrupted Natalie when she asked him not to do so. He also knew he was identifying with Spencer's shock that Natalie thought only of punishment. The red of the story made Waverly's mind spin, and brought the voice of Cynthia. *Let there be wild*, she might have said. He took a sip of cold coffee, realizing again, there is no such thing as neutral. By the time he set his cup down, he was calm enough to ask a question.

"What else came spilling out when you argued about the incident with Bryce? Mind you, I'm not asking for a replay."

Waverly was thinking about tornadoes. Some folks remember the moment when the hinges came off a storm door and they were huddling in a corner. Others remember only the silence after it passed, or a portrait of devastation. Waverly's mentors stressed a hundred times to pay attention to how each person listens, or doesn't, while the other is talking, and to appreciate the way emotions speak from the body.

"Well, Natalie said, we came back to the kitchen and started screaming at each other. I can't even remember what I said."

Spencer was patient for a microsecond, and then he pounced, surprising everyone, even Frog.

"Of course you can't remember. You're not that interested in Bryce unless she's in trouble. She's not a doll you dress up and put away. Sometimes you scold her like a bad dog. These are the most magical years of a child's life and you won't even try to play with her. There's no pretend in you. There's no child in you."

Natalie replied, "I admit it. I was pissed and I had an immediate reaction. I went too far. I was raised being told how to behave, that the important thing in life is to get right answers and not cause trouble for my parents." She faced Spencer at an obtuse angle, preparing to fire back.

"How would you know my world with Natalie? She has a serious side she never shows you. You get to be all fun, all the time. I work as hard as you and make dinner five nights straight without a recent thank you. You come home and watch the evening news. With Bryce, you're all about play. You could offer to bring home dinner. Plus you think everything Bryce does is golden, and everything I do is expected. Where's my praise, Mr. Spar…?"

She caught herself from mentioning the nickname and almost changed it to say *Mr. Spencer,* but of course it was too late. She screamed it in her mind, and the intention splashed all over Spencer in a Jackson Pollock way.

"What am I missing? Spencer asked her. "This is all news to me, that you feel this way."

"You're missing just about everything," Natalie trailed off, on the downslope of trying to explain.

Waverly was relieved to have gotten to the raw narrative. Addressing Natalie, he said, "Please go on about the everything." To his infinite surprise, Natalie's response was to begin caressing her upper thigh with her index finger, making perfect little circles. Frog saw it clearly from above. For the first time since he was carved from a tree, he wished he had a mate.

"You see, Dr. Waverly, I was a person who made very few mistakes; I pride myself on that carefulness. This guy on the couch next to me takes my hints as meaningless. I want him to go back to when he wanted more of me, not less. I suppose I get tired of trying."

She explained her mother was chronically depressed, with a sterile elevation of order; a style so compressed that Natalie had to glean her mother's moods from the way she put away dishes. The screech of a kitchen drawer could ruin her mother's day. Her father left when she was twelve. Natalie didn't have a choice to leave. At meals, passions and joys of the day were suspect, as if they needed to be herded like stray sheep. She was trapped in her mother's unhappiness.

"Dr. Waverly, are there rules in your office? Like what would you do if I asked my husband to give me oral sex right now on the couch? Then you could see what happens, and more to the point, what doesn't happen. A man should take his time."

Waverly was astounded by her comment, and even suspected that Frog might have had a hand in nudging her to speak from her dream version. It's just the kind of thing Frog liked to do to stir things up, and then pretend all innocent, like he's just a wooden artifact with no awareness at all. But the version of Natalie in front of him really said it, and Waverly was unprepared for her drawing him in, until he remembered having followed her into the portrait.

She laughed a little bit. "Don't worry, I'm more private than that. It's just that other men wanted so little from me in the past, to feel me up, trying to get me drunk for a little sex. I'd go along, but it wasn't like I was really there. I suppose I never explored what I wanted. My role was to play along."

"There's more to that observation, isn't there?" Waverly couldn't resist.

She frowned and wouldn't speak, but chose the moment to locate Spencer, who was clearly drowning. She admitted it was delicious that he used to be so curious about her, and she admitted to loving the boy in the man. In Waverly's translation, each wanted some foothold of recognition, some vestige of the original feeling of connection, but the path was overgrown with blackberry vines that cut the skin for reaching. Natalie opened the floodgates.

"Look, I've told you before. Spencer, I don't like you pouting and sighing when you want sex. I want sex too, even lust sometimes, and other times I like you lingering. A little prelude and nuance would be nice, but you make yourself forlorn and pathetic, acting like I'm simply cold if I don't jump to the moment."

Spencer stood up right there in the room, enraged.

"Don't you see the half-truth in that? You get to be punitive one minute, seductive or cold the next, and whatever I do, I'm locked out if I don't read the tea leaves perfectly."

Frog saw Spencer's desperation and signaled the shame of it to Waverly. There was a time when Frog himself had imagined a poisoned pond. Spencer continued on a resonant D note, for his voice was baritone.

"No matter how I reach for you in bed, the last five times you've said you're just getting to the good part of your book. That doesn't exactly encourage me."

Natalie was caught off-guard, and tried to save face, saying, "It's true I read a lot of very good books, but it's also true that when you come to bed, you open your laptop to see what's happening in the Asian stock market. We're both sensitive. We're both noticing each other while locked in our stupid habits. Will you give me that?"

Waverly fancied these two as masters of mutual avoidance, locked in a familiar trap. She felt Spencer missed every hint of her growing unhappiness. He protested that she refuses to say what she wants or doesn't want. She said the need to explain was equivalent to shame in her family. Around and around they went.

Frog was thinking, *humans don't realize that frogs have dreams too, and not just ones where they catch a dragonfly. I've fallen for a human woman. I never thought it possible.*

Waverly looked to the left just then, because that's what he does when he needs help. Natalie was there, and Cynthia McBride was next to her. What had he missed about his own marriage? His thoughts careened down a narrow tidal passage until he remembered a comment from one of his perceptive mentors, the incredible Elizabeth Mars.

"Wait until a fresh emotion shows itself, first darkly on the horizon. It will glimmer in the distance and brighten suddenly. You'll know by the rushing sound that you're close to a waterfall." Waverly thought, *I'm already over the waterfall. What now?*

Then the husband from the dream whispered in Waverly's other ear, from another part of the bookcase.

"Ask her to speak in the math kind of way. It's our familiar language." Again, Waverly refused to obey the foreign voice, but in the interim, the couple descended into a spiral of accusations and cross-complaints. Sometimes in therapy, well, all the time actually, you see the child in the adult. Natalie must have sensed the whisper, because she said to her husband, "You haven't even noticed the downward slope of my mood."

Spencer, now sitting but still upset, countered by saying, "I can't respond unless you give me some parameters."

"How's this for a parameter?" Natalie gave him the finger, a first in their marriage, surprising herself to such a degree her hand stayed in the air for a full five seconds. Spencer plunged into a pool of sarcasm.

"Thanks for being honest, dear. Can you put that in words longer than two for Dr. Waverly?"

"This is for you, dear husband, and all the things you expect of me that I can't possibly do." At this, Spencer was genuinely sad. He thought of reminding her that he loved her, hoping it would be enough. Magic words were left unsaid and he was relieved at finally having her full attention. After all, he had complaints too.

FIRE AND ICE

Collecting himself, Spencer said to his wife, "I'm a man who can genuinely love and be faithful. I know I'm a work in progress, but I won't let you turn me into your father, who gave up and left the scene. Just remember, I never needed you to be perfect. That was always your assumption, not mine."

Waverly entertained the possibility that Spencer had just made the worst possible reference a human can make in the middle of an argument: don't bring parents into it. But Spencer was in a gambling mood, with all the cards on the table. He also remembered that juice resides in the risky thing. Frog saw a whirlpool open on the beige carpet. It nearly took all of them in. Briefly, Frog wanted to be human so he could finally groan out loud. The feeling quickly passed. Then Natalie from the dream whispered to both men in the room.

"I want to be kidnapped to the north of Hadrian's Wall, to where the barbarians live." Frog, as keeper of blind spots, saw Spencer's dilemma, and also saw what was coming. It's a dirty trick to out your partner about something embarrassing in front of a new therapist, but Spencer decided to risk it, telling Natalie he was well aware she'd been watching porn where the women are frenzied, having sex with strangers, in public, in closets, dressing rooms of stores, the back seats of cars, sometimes with multiple men. Always, the ripping of clothes, the anonymity, the risk of being caught. He dreaded the possible meanings. It made him sad, as if he barely knew his wife. He wanted to be the stranger in her desires. For their first year together, there was always a trail of clothes on the floor. They had sex everywhere but in bed. He wondered, out loud, if she had a lover or possibly several.

"How dare you look at my computer? She said. "It's just pretend, I don't really want to act it out with strangers." Nobody spoke for a long, long time. She changed her tone, saying, "I drifted into that because you, I mean me, I…oh shit, I don't know why I do it. It's easy I suppose. I'm not having sex with anybody if that's your concern. Are you trying to tell me you've never looked at porn?"

"Not your kind, that's for sure. Don't turn this around so soon, Nat. I've been afraid to ask if you're really wanting out. I'm not interested in keeping a fake marriage together for the sake of Bryce. Not interested at all. If you're acting out some script where you suffer deprivation with me and play out your desires with strangers, I'm not up for that. You give me zero credit for trying to change that script."

Stop this madness, thought Frog, getting impatient with humans. *What good does it do to explain suffering in these ways?* Frog had a wish he never conveyed to Waverly; that he longs to become petrified wood at the bottom of an alpine lake and stay for a thousand years. When the lake becomes a meadow, he hopes that humans aren't around. Reptiles and insects can rule. He never asked to be carved in the shape of a frog anyway, never agreed to the role of watcher. Out in the air like this, wood doesn't last forever. Pine is soft, vulnerable. Now that he's been given a purpose, he'll do it in his own way. It's just that he can't imagine being released to water until he's hardened and will surely sink. If released now, he'd only float and be picked off and shredded for the nest of a great blue heron.

The tide was out for Spencer Mason. He feared he'd lost his wife, that she would announce it in the next few minutes. Waverly saw the possibility too, and wondered if Natalie had stayed too long in the portrait, or if he was daydreaming them into a script of his own. She surprised them both, saying it was she who prodded Spencer into calling for the appointment, even though he was the one to call. But she said it like a child. She said it like she was announcing there's no candy hidden behind the art books on the third shelf.

The Final Fifteen

In that moment, for better or worse, Waverly made a comment that was completely unfiltered and hadn't risen to a thought.

"The driving force of our curiosity doesn't emerge until we live in the turbulent messiness of another person trying to know us. I feel you're both very close."

To this, Spencer nodded in a special way, looking over the rim of his glasses at such an angle, his world was re-positioned. Natalie was confused, but attentive. She liked the reference to the word *messy* for the first time in her life.

Spencer was nearly ruined by then, but some vestige of him survived.

"Give me a break," fumed Natalie, "talk to me directly, as if I'm in the room."

"But you're not, my dear, you're not really in the room," Spencer responded.

Then she reached to touch his shoulder, but in the reach, she was not the same person at all. A cloud entered the consulting room, obscuring all parties with white gauze. Another presence entered Natalie's body. The presence spoke, but only to Spencer.

"Spencer, Sparky, it's me, Lucien, the one who gave you your nickname. I still love you. Don't ask me to explain it. I don't know why I'm here. I dreamt I followed a mystic frog to find you. I wanted to marry you when I was seven. Let's not analyze this. Don't tell Dr. Waverly, he won't get it. Look at him, he's lost in his portrait. I want you to know I'm married to a wonderful guy. I can see you love this woman. Don't be a dope. Apologize when you're being a jerk. Stop acting pathetic. Keep it simple. Touch her the way she likes."

The apparition left the room, leaving Spencer stunned, the others numb. One of the few certainties in Waverly's mind was that they were running low on time. He offered regular sessions to go into other regions. Spencer looked at Natalie, "Sweetheart, tell me if we can repair this, and how?"

"Oh no you don't," Natalie said. "See, Dr. Waverly, this is what he does, putting it back on me. It's lazy. I've come to distrust the *sweetheart* word. Notice he didn't make any suggestions. Don't you guys see paradox on the menu?"

"What menu?" asked Spencer, while Frog smiled his wooden best.

"What paradox?" asked Waverly.

"Don't you see, this is just a subtle guilt trip on *me*. Spelling things out to men is the opposite of what I want. It's like we're at a restaurant and we can all read the menu, but I find myself having to read it and ask what everybody wants. I resent the feeling."

"So don't ever do it again," offered Spencer. "I'm not the one to make you feel that way. I never asked you to feel that way." He was dumbfounded.

Waverly thought, *this pair speaks a nullifying language. Both experience the visceral trap the other is trying to avoid.*

"You guys are impossible," Natalie continued. "It's my turn to tell a story. We were talking the other day and I told Spencer I was mildly to moderately depressed and he didn't even care. He asked, with irritation, 'Which is it, mildly or moderately?' Can you think of anything more maddening?"

Spencer tried to defend himself, but failed to the nth degree. "You know I hate it when you can't make that distinction. You devise math tests that rely on statistical sampling, but you won't even try to use precise terms with me. It keeps me in the dark, helpless. There's no calculus for the derivatives of your failure to be more specific."

She wasn't finished. "I'm telling you my truth and you're not listening. I'm somewhere between those two categories." It was her turn to fall apart and appeal to Waverly.

"Spencer told me he was stressed to the asymptote when he knows I'm haunted by that graph, how it never really reaches an end. I won't let him do that. He can't imply a category that we haven't agreed on. Please help."

Waverly was genuinely confused, certain of only one thing—that he'd entered the dream again, where the couple spoke only in math language. He began to ask a question, then Spencer interrupted, putting his hands to the sides of his face, ignoring Waverly, pleading to his wife.

"Just say it! You think I'm some version of the null hypothesis and you're trying like hell to prove it."

Natalie backed off, stammering. "If I'm so invalid, why do you have to raise your voice. Keep this up and I'll go outlier on you (a reference to an unusual number in a statistical sample which can distort norms and conclusions). Of course we're valid, look at us, two people having an argument. If you recall, it was you who needed to quantify every goddamned thing under the sun when I met you. I can't believe I thought it was cute. I was interested in the promise of you. I had no idea the sacrifice I was making. It weakened us. Here's my promise; I'll never refer to categories again, and let's see if you're man enough to handle it. I came here because I'm like a black hole, with infinite density, ready to explode. None of my light can escape."

"Me too," said Spencer. He was irritated that his wife had stolen the same metaphor he was about to use. All he could do was gesture to Waverly, as if the doctor could fix everything in a few sentences. When hope dissolved, he broke down and softly asked; "Why didn't you tell me you were so miserable? I'm not the equation you fear. You're right. Something weakened us and we can start right there."

Natalie took the bait with renewed vigor.

"This isn't the time for calculus, why don't you want me like you used to?"

"I do. I do. I always want to grab you. It's always on my mind. You can't hug a cactus, you know very well what I mean."

UNVEILING

In that moment, Waverly felt the dream was both his and theirs. *They're an American mosaic,* he thought, more complicated than he or Frog could fathom. He surrendered to their blend of formality, war, and desire.

Frog knew the larger story. After his wife died, Waverly saw frozen couples everywhere, even in reflections of store windows. He watched, non-blinking, as Waverly spoke to the couple.

"I'd like to end by drawing you both back to what your daughter asked, about the red line up the wall, and what that moment evoked."

"Oh that," said Natalie, "we painted it over."

Spencer chimed in, "The hell we did. Three coats of paint, but if you get up close, you'll see that red streak is still there."

Nobody spoke for a full minute.

"I know we're out of time," Spencer said, "I don't want to end there. There's something I need to say to Natalie." He turned, as if delivering the most important line of his life. "You are a continuous variable, not the discrete variable I've been taking you for."

Without looking up, Natalie responded with hideous blandness and the hint of a wicked grin.

"Cut the crap, Mr. Math, you are so guilty of a Type One logical error, I can't even believe you earned your Ph.D. Are you going to take me to bed or not?"

"You really don't want to go there with me on the math analogies. I'll crush you."

"Try me…in bed I mean. Don't beg, just act, as if we just met and I'm the strange girl you can't get enough of. By the way, I have to ask something important. You've been saying the name *Lucien* in your sleep for two years. Now that we're coming clean, tell me who she is. She's not still in your life is she?"

Spencer (Sparky) Mason was shaken, but did not speak of his visitation. It was way too hard to explain. Frog gave him a lifeline, a solution, since Waverly was far away. Spencer offered his wife a nickname. He wanted it to be *Zirna*, Etruscan Goddess of the waxing moon.

"And so it is," she mused, looking first at her husband, then at Frog in the bookshelf. "I'm going to have to think on a new one for you, or rather *Zirna* will." She had a thought to run away with Frog, but that was a fairy tale.

Alone with a Covered Portrait

They left the scene with an agreement to meet again, leaving Waverly in the last natural light of day. It cut through his blinds while he stood in the center of his consulting room. The soft light kindled him to go home and uncover the piece Cynthia was working on when she died. He wasn't afraid of it anymore. For the first time, he liked the idea it was unfinished. Cynthia was rarely obscure without purpose. In that exact moment, he gave Frog a proper name.

"Good night, Spud, and good work today." A light flickered in the hallway.

At home, Waverly lifted the cloth covering Cynthia's final painting and saw a red line cutting through graphic blues and grays. It cut through all his assumptions and he found it beautiful, separating want from fear, not a scream, more a stream of lava running down to a hissing sea. Close up, it became an adagio, but from distance, an allegro.

The red line ventured off the edge of the canvas, travelling five inches up the easel, making it clear she intended the easel as part of the piece. All year, he was puzzled as to where to mount the painting, thinking only of a favored wall. A strange awareness rushed him, more a presence than a thought. Kicking off his shoes, grabbing a bit of scotch, no ice, he went looking for a place where the easel and painting would never be parted. In a breath of air, a gulp of scotch, he found the perfect corner.

Looking out from his apartment window, Waverly offered a nod to the endless sirens of the streets of Manhattan. It was pointless to look for their source. The sounds were obscured by buildings and echoed off too many places: muted, amplified, no longer sharp, rising to combine his grief and great relief, in a version of one plus one.

A Perfect Stillness

While posing for a portrait class, Catalina Ortega had a revelation. She'd mastered a perfect stillness, but a curtain enclosing her space began to fall, allowing a patch of unfiltered light to spill across her oval face. Falling things always spoke to Catalina. Instead of being startled, as others were, she smiled in private acceptance; the kind a child finds when no one is around. The feeling was not surrender, not resignation, more like the awareness of a breeze when someone out of sight opens a window. A similar moment occurred during her orientation for modeling, when her eighty-year-old teacher spoke from a wheelchair to remind everyone that the care of light is essential. It has to be reflected off screens, measured, and considered for angles, with reverence for the skin. The delicate woman leaned toward Catalina and singled her out with a minimal voice, as if she knew her in another life.

"Unlike the outer world, everything gets to be soft in the studio, controlled, with a hint of the unreal. The model can go anywhere during the pose, anywhere at all."

The renegade curtain was quickly replaced but Catalina took the moment as a message. The ardent students didn't notice her transformation. Now she was a study in prescience, no longer a distant figure. They were too busy with their sighs, mixing colors, sitting so close to her in a semi-circle she could sense their strokes and frowns. Her eyes held fast to the moment, fixed on an aging elm, outside, where light is free.

The breeze remained inside her, as if the old woman was still with her, guarding the open window, allowing Catalina to see her own life from both sides of the curtain. She wondered if the students missed her essence, but realized it's difficult to paint eyes that are searching for another life. It bothered her that she was often painted as vacant, and she finally had to admit the hardest truth of all; sometimes that's how she posed. Maybe the students were spot on and she was the last to see. Still, she hated the moment when they trapped her in some dismal, wanting frame. Birch was wrong in every way and white oak had no conversation with her skin.

She wandered down the hall of the thought, catching herself midway. The students were beginners. What did she expect? It's a rare gift to render a person with any accuracy at all. It was her thirty-fifth birthday, and for her wish, she wanted to step forward in her life and run away with the elusive treasure. Ten minutes remained before her sitting was over. In the ten, then the nine, she recalled the last time she felt so misperceived. It was five years ago, in the middle of her divorce, in the middle of a therapy session. She felt reduced to an affection-starved child in a woman's body, nothing more than a lost soul in need of an endless maternal voice. Her therapist had country cottages on office walls, and insisted that Catalina needed only to cry and be held. The cottages turned into prisons and she was locked in one. She left without any closure. *Whose need was that?* She asked herself, looking back on the insistent touch, retreating to her doubts. A student coughed and it brought her back. Time was up. Most of the students had left. She hurried home in a fog.

Saturday brought the wind. Crisp October air raked the Sacramento morning, biting her cheeks in shadows of stately trees in the arboretum of Capitol Park. Normally she did not walk briskly, and studied the shapes of trees, but her steps quickened when she heard the bells of the Cathedral of the Blessed Sacrament. She went to give thanks for the gift of her seven-year-old daughter, Miranda.

In the church, in the land of echoes, she looked at one hand, then the other, wondering when they would join to pray. Instead, they parted, and lifted her from the pew. She looked up high, but the new stained glass was too bright, too ethereal, so she resumed her walk instead of attending Mass at noon. The bench at Cesar Chavez Park was the better kind, exposed in every season, gleaming, waiting, washed by a recent rain.

She fixed her eyes on children at play and imagined being among them. In that instant she decided to give up modeling. The universe answered by turning a single leaf at her feet. Even if it was just the wind, the fresh colors on the underside brought her almost to a smile. It's risky to think there are messages for you everywhere, but Catalina felt secure in the decision. Before she could change her mind, she called the studio on her cell, to give them notice and agree to one last pose. She touched her fingers one-by-one against her thumb in a sequence she kept secret, and waited for images to flow. She invented the ritual in childhood, as a summoning or a soothing.

In summoning, it brought her grandfather, Miguel. He loved reading to her in Spanish until he died when she was five. She would restore him, find the one photograph in the wooden crate, and bring Miguel to an honored shelf so he could read to her forever. In soothing, it brought her dance teacher from high school, the one who squared her shoulders, saw the need for motion, and made her promise to never stop dancing. The thought made her look at her solemn her feet and resolve to dance again—the opposite of posing.

Her memories were lucid and the bench was a rift in time. Soon, a man named Che approached her mind. He was not in the park, but she knew how to make it so, imagining him on a nearby bench where she could paint him into her life. If she read him right from their brief encounters, locking eyes while shopping, he was keen on her, and wanted her to know.

She studied his casual confidence from memory: faded blue blazer, black polished shoes, jeans that fit, recent shave, lean, with humor in the eyes, seriousness in the brow, steps not so light as a bounce, more a small transcendence. Cuban, she thought, or Spanish, or Argentinian—a mix of spice and formality. Maria, being a bank manager, noticed the smaller signs, like the way a person holds a pen before applying a signature, not to mention the revelation in a scribble. She always noticed the slant, the loops above and below the signature line, the place where a *t* is crossed, how far the *g* dips into the underworld. She could see a person's playfulness, kindness, aggression too, by the push of a shopping cart.

If her senses were on target, Che was neither maniac nor monk, gliding along in a mix of determination and impulse. He would not be predictable, not meticulous either. He would rail at the sky if angered, but not harm the people close to him. It was a relief she didn't know him from art class or the bank. Desire has a taste, even from far away. It was delicious to Catalina that everything he knew about her was right there in his eyes.

Thirty new moons had filled the sky since she'd been approached by a man with such a tempting blend of masculinity and reserve. It brought a crisp sensation. She filled her lungs and it brought him closer, to the skin and deeper places. She remembered how Che brightened in the sweetest way when she gave her ancient smile on their second meeting in the market. No words then. None seemed right. She saw him again a few weeks later and froze the anxious moment, resolving to unfold it like a map during her final pose for art class.

In the stillness of her final pose, she fell to a wanting mood, but this time she gave a nod of encouragement to students, as if to say they could find her in their paintings and she wouldn't block her essence.

In the last half-hour she cast a fantasy. Yes, she would take a salsa dance class. Che would happen to be there. She knew the smooth, sexy combinations from long ago, since they never leave your mind. He'd be rusty at first, respectful, and roles of lead and follow would disappear in the hypnotic rhythms. They would practice until his open hand on her back was just the way she wanted, solid, fingers slightly spread, firm, not tentative. She'd reply by anchoring her fingers tightly to the back of his shoulder, and her other hand would meet him in a daring show of strength, surprising him just a little. Heaven in a frame. He would intuit when she wanted to spin, and would not be the kind who commanded. And spin she would, as if the child in her was released to an April breeze. Her return to him would be even sweeter, for salsa carries secrets in the homecoming of a spin. The rest of the world could vanish.

The quietness was good, the curtain held, and the light gave thanks from above. She would miss the drifting hours. The old woman was right in every way about the care of light.

During the long walk home, she stopped at the roses in McKinley Park. Stopping was always risky when she was full of hope. *Who am I kidding?* she thought. Nightmares from childhood haunted her the minute she allowed herself to dream. She found another bench; one that invited her personally. There in the park, in the flat city of trees, she was close to the merging rivers. The Sacramento is slow, muddy from silt from the north. The American River is clear and cold, fresh from the Sierra Nevada, with a parkway second to none.

The sound of a nearby siren breached a levee in her mind. She could never tell Che her story. His image flew from the bench like a frightened heron, leaving her to fill the moats of her castle with the last of her tears. She wanted to open the drawbridge to her life, but it was stuck; memories were like boulders, clogging up the gears. She decided to give therapy another try. Probably there would be just one meeting, but it was her birthday and she promised.

Attentive hands of a sensitive man were not on Catalina's mind as she sat down with Jason Quinn. She found him on the internet, where therapists say a bit about their training and approach. He said something about a mix of art and science, the importance of stories and attachments, not just symptoms. His photo offered his eyes, but didn't show his hands.

When she settled into her chair, she wasn't aware that her hands were already telling her story. Jason thought he saw one hand trying to scream as it clutched the arm of her chair. The other was fixed in a defiant fist, a lump of clay in her lap.

His hands were involved with hers from the very first moment, from across the room, across a raging river. Even if these two tried to yell in the customary ways, cupping hands to mouths, carefully aiming the voice, the river was too swift and loud, and all their words were swept to sea from a hundred miles inland.

To Catalina, Jason's left hand seemed open and optimistic, with fingers stretched over his thigh. His right hand looked constricted, trapped and tucked under his chin, as if it guarded mournful knowledge. In the space of a dozen breaths, their four hands didn't move. That's what the Japanese lamp would say. It was not a standoff, more a conversation. Jason's fingers embarked on a minimal rise and fall. Catalina remembered whispering to herself when making the appointment, *he'll hear of hands that harmed me. He'll be the first man I've told.*

She scanned the man, the same man who touched her in the waiting room with a welcome handshake. No fear there, no crushing grip. His desk had stacks of books. Opposite, a collection of vases resided in a curved section of his bookcase. She fixed on a flower arrangement in an ikebana bowl, aglow with clusters of miniature climbing roses leaning slightly apart—all that white in a forest of reeds, backed by leaves of ironwood. It was not Japanese at all, but was not haphazard either. It reminded Catalina of a huge tree she saw as a child, split by lightning, both parts still alive. It occurred to her how much she was like the tree.

Her right hand could have been a stop sign, refusing all the images. But her left hand took the lead, allowing two fingers to extend, as if touching the water of Jason's presence.

More silence followed, then a shared image of a pool below. Leaping, they held their breath, but not each other. Catalina found she could speak underwater, as long as words could just be bubbles. Jason was allowed to read her lips; that's all. It was forbidden to read emotions. He asked her to begin anywhere she wanted.

She surprised herself with her opening comments, telling of her father's death when she was ten, although he was a drifter since she was two. The news stripped her of hope that he'd come back, and rekindled her fear that she was defective, or he wouldn't have left in the first place. Such is a child's belief.

"I have a hobby studying great divides," she said, before Jason formed a question. "I'm fascinated by Berlin in the cold war, the breakup of the USSR, Korea even now, and civil wars in every country. My divorce was five years ago, so was my last therapy. My world is my daughter and I love my work as a banker. In banking, things get to be neat. I can leave the day behind as long as the numbers match. I take care of potted plants when I'm down. I've been on antidepressants, they helped me for a time, a safety net when I was falling, but I don't want them anymore. They also made me numb."

Jason was looking for breadcrumbs when she circled around to Che.

"There's this man. His name is Che. I fear I like him, but I'm not ready for a new man in my life." It was an irony not lost on Jason, since he was as new to her as a shiny coin. Jason nodded his curious best, privately wondering why she chose to see a male therapist. But it's something of a crime to interrupt the flow in therapy.

She told him how Che had noticed her in a market before she spotted him. She was touching the vegetables and fruit, sampling them for the right blend of color, give, and texture, but didn't expect to be noticed. The second she realized he was watching, she felt he knew too much, and her split became a chasm. She recalled the moment of panic.

"I said out loud, under my breath, *what do I want to happen here?* It was the weirdest moment. I never talk to myself out loud. What does it mean when you talk to yourself out loud, Dr. Quinn?"

She didn't want an answer and was glad he didn't try. Next, she was standing in the checkout line with Che directly behind. He offered an awkward comment, but she liked the hope in his voice. They chanced to meet that way again, and he asked her out for coffee. She said yes, in a hypothetical way, but didn't give a day.

"Dr. Quinn, it bothers me that something this natural could be so terrifying."

A place for thinking came to Jason's mind, by the American River, on a bench overlooking the magnificent scene. He could fix on the v-shaped trails made by Canada Geese in the water, or the circles made by turtles coming to the surface. The riparian banks are rich with cottonwoods and oaks, drawing him in every season. He imagined Catalina in the landscape, just out of view, on the far side of a small island.

Back in the room, Catalina's voice did not gather, did not act like a voice at all, more a scattering of syllables in monotone. Her hands were crossed, making a perfect X in her lap, palm over wrist, fingers pointing to opposite walls. She didn't know where to go. Jason felt his own version of a chasm, but thought of a bridge instead, and asked if she would describe her home.

He liked it when she took a moment to look at the art on his office walls (a Japanese teahouse, landscapes, trees, abstract rivers), as if to insist on knowing the person asking. She pointed to a path in one of his landscapes, offering a half-smile, like she might go there for a walk sometime. With no connection of their eyes, she told him her kitchen had posters from every continent, from tropical forests to glaciers, with deserts in between. But a frown appeared on the edges of her mouth, along with a small recovery, hinting that she wished she could start over, for she'd told a little lie.

She thought of not telling him that she'd destroyed two entire continents in a rage, ripped them from the wall and left the spaces blank. Her daughter saw the whole thing. It was hard enough to explain to Miranda, a bad day and all, but even Miranda knew that wasn't the truth of the moment. When she repeated the story to Jason, it was diluted, as if it happened years ago, not last week—as if it had no connection to personal rage, just rage in general, just something that happened.

"I'm always filling spaces," Catalina said, "I'll make perfectly even spaces between my potted plants, lining them up in a nice little row. Perhaps I should try arranging them in clusters. Maybe I won't get so mad."

He had the strangest image of a jewelry box hidden in her kitchen, and was thinking how boxes hold treasures. He conjured up a photo of Catalina as a child. Surely someone had drawn her long ago in sidewalk chalk and taken a photo. She was skipping rope with joy, around the age of seven. He placed the imagined photo in the imagined jewelry box. All she did to make it so was glance at a cedar box where he kept his favorite pens. Already, their worlds were mingling.

Of course she didn't give more history. Not yet. She was thinking how the world opens in perception, narrows in description, surrenders to imagination.

Jason was stunned when he saw how her eyes were like other people's hands, tracing the shapes of vases on the far shelf. It could have come to a question, but silence was the road. The moment was made of silk, and he had the urge to ask her, ever so delicately, what caught her eye so keenly. But to ask about such things would remove him from the edges of her frown, so he laid his questions down.

She continued to describe her home, ushering him to her living room, where it felt to Jason she was erasing all the colors of a brilliant tropical bird, pointing to a loveseat and chairs, a television and a rug, as if there was no such thing as color. She tried to make the room seem plain, like a wooden spoon or a square white napkin.

Jason knew she was not plain. He saw it when her fingers took a languid walk across her knees. Briefly, before she offered more, he remembered visiting a period mansion in France, where rooms are roped-off from visitors. You could lean over the rope, but an alarm would signal if you entered. One room stood out—a small room with old furniture and even older rugs. A walnut desk featured a single piece of paper and a fountain pen. The room was made to look as if the occupant had been writing something, and had left the chair askew. Alone at the rope, Jason could strain all he wanted, but couldn't read what was there. It might have been an invitation, a sonnet, a litany or a plea. The dim lamp would not release a meaning.

Catalina lightened when she described her daughter's room—a monument to protection and play—with dolls of every description, soccer shin guards on the floor, a hamster on a wheel, and posters of dogs and turtles. Jason was a father too, which he revealed by a knowing grin in response to the query in her brow, nothing more than a flash of recognition. There was no reason to be obscure. They smiled at the images she described, also the ones presumed, while Catalina continued down the hall toward the other rooms.

From the soft office chair, she described her study, filled with books of art. He felt such vibrancy there, where colors were allowed to live. A section of her desk was reserved for mail and bills. A guitar gathered dust in the corner, and photographs of fields of wheat were scattered on the floor, hoping for a wall. Another corner held a globe with pins in the countries she'd visited. Jason was captive, realizing she allowed him to see the different places by making small turns of her wrist; each turn opened an image to him, just a little, before moving her hand back to the X position, while he became, since she invited, a better listener than he was before.

"My bedroom is a mess. I don't make the bed very often, maybe once a week. I have intentions, but I stand or sit there in the morning looking at the portrait of a storm over my bed. It's brimming in the whites of waves. The grays and blues are savage, but the edge has lighter blue coming out of the charcoal-colored night, with a little pink here and there, like the hint of a clearing sky. Sometimes I see the storm going right over the edge of the frame, rushing toward me. I've been late to work because I couldn't leave it. Please, doctor, don't say the obvious. I suppose since I put it there, the portrait is some version of me, or what happened to me, but I don't really want to know, and I don't want you to know, either." She folded her arms, surprised at what she said.

"I trust you've always had a very private way of knowing."

"I told you about one one-hundredth, and I already regret it. That's enough for now."

Jason wanted a hundredth more, for she was the scent of lime. She saw his hands relax, as if to receive a gift, but her gift was to herself, extending her arm toward the window, fingers unfurling like an evening primrose. It was rare for Jason to be as patient as the moon. Therapists try to be patient. It doesn't mean they are. He knew to look out the window. It seemed to be her one condition for saying more.

"My bedspread has a pattern of gentle waves. It's a quilt I won at a fair. My walls are painted in Snip of Tannin. It's a pretty sort of beige. I'm thinking of painting the room maroon, but it's a bit too close to red."

In response, Jason's fingers found each other at the tips, not the palms, and they settled in his lap. His thumbs were touching, which was often his way of looking at the universe. If viewed from above, they formed an arch, but from Catalina's angle, he was pointing a prayer toward sorrows she hadn't told.

He wanted to linger in the rooms and toss the clock out the window. He imagined reading a book with her under a giant oak; a breeze would turn the page when it was time. There was only one rule in the daydream: they couldn't speak about what they were reading. The feeling was like a sip of wine that opens, and opens again. All the books and art in his office, the zinnias and the ebony vase, came alive from their background places, like tension building in a Beethoven symphony.

Jason recalled the words of one of his favorite mentors, Dr. Elizabeth Mars. She turned ninety not long ago, but refused to celebrate. *If you tame the need to rescue, others can use you as a real person. Never rush the unfolding of a moment with the crudeness of an interview.*

With Catalina in his presence, Jason was thinking of the hooded oriole that visits his yard from time to time—skittish, with a habit of returning the moment he looks away. He turns and she is there. He looks and she is gone.

Catalina was shaken by an apparition and switched to a strident tone, announcing she decided long ago she was not going to be miserable. It was then she told him why she came: she couldn't make peace with her own skin, and dreaded the slightest unexpected touch. It wasn't always that way. She told him about her previous therapy, the touches there, the cottages.

"Dancing is different," she said. "There are frames, hand-switches, sequences, accepted areas of connection. Of course, posing for an art class is not about touch at all. I suppose that's why it felt safe."

"Did something happen that made you stop dancing?"

Suddenly she started to retch, becoming pale right there in the session. He offered a glass of water. She nodded in acceptance. Both had to reach to make the exchange.

"Can touch ever feel safe after you've been used and thrown away? I don't want to waste my time or yours if the answer is *no*. I can live like this if I have to. I've done it most of my life."

Jason hesitated, then spoke as if his suddenly self-conscious hands were his best advisors. "I believe you'll surprise yourself with your determination. I'll ask you to tell me what you notice in the moment, regardless of where it leads. Please include sensations, images, vignettes, even what you see in me."

"Well, there was my mother's complete lack of protection, the absence of a father, a litany of selfish men, my habit of rejecting decent men, a period of heavy drinking, my leadership on boards and charities, a volatile, hurtful marriage, a girlfriend experiment that ended very badly. My only trust right now is with my daughter, and recently, the cello." She mentioned the elegant embrace of wood, how she loves to hold the bow in the air before drawing it against the strings.

"I'm in love with the long, deep tones of the cello. When I'm playing, my whole body vibrates. My teacher used to play in the San Francisco Symphony. I had no idea you can play a note that goes on forever once you learn to change the direction of the bow without pausing. I can't believe it took thirty-five years to find the instrument right for me."

On their second meeting, Catalina got herself a cup of water from the waiting room and gulped every drop in the hallway before making it to her chair. She did not want to accept a pattern where Jason would bring her water.

"So I had the stupid coffee date with Che. I faked it, couldn't relax in the slightest, only talked about my work at the bank. I want to go back to posing for art students. Portrait students don't talk, they don't ask questions, and I don't have to do anything. I don't think I said one meaningful thing to Che. At one point I shuddered uncontrollably and he gave me his jacket. It was eighty-five degrees outside. At the end he wanted to give me a hug, and I wanted it too, but my skin wouldn't allow me to respond. So he gave the one-arm kind of hug you get from the host of a party where they never bothered to learn your name. I turned away as if

I was cold, but I'm not a cold person. I swear, Che barely knows me but he's already confused. My body is saying something isn't right, but it's never right. I'm so sick of me!"

For a minute, maybe longer, she stared at a tall blue vase.

Her way of looking was a study in itself; a reluctant need, with sadness at the edge of futility. The tone was not missed on Jason, who found himself back in her home, in the study, where a rhyme came to him: *something dissociated, something sweet, a private thought, a field of wheat.* Dr. Elizabeth Mars made one of her famous visitations to his mind. She was fond of saying, *people tell you, without even knowing it, how they can be helped.* He wanted the paradoxes, the long shadows of Catalina.

A sudden flip of Catalina's hand woke him, uncannily, to a very different scene. What kind of magic did she have? He saw the exact way she would throw a bowl of rice across the room, the red way she would glare at her hands in anger. He saw her as a troubled teen, trying to put the full weight of her presence on a table with only three legs. But he also saw her struggling not to hide everything. The images hid in a lemon bush, along with a handful of sparrows.

She filled him in a little more; a past runner of marathons, a sister who never calls, an older brother in prison, relatives in Nicaragua. She was a student of languages, wild in the kitchen, but practical as a bank manager. Nobody would suspect the contrasts.

"I also love rivers, uncommon fences, shadows at 6:00 P.M., Beethoven, Stravinsky, and Bach, along with salsa and bachata." Her grandparents brought the family to California. The artifacts burned in a fire.

Jason made his own private additions: quick glances, elusive beauty, not the high cheeks of nobility, not an ounce of aloof. Determined, solid chin, skin like the smooth bark of manzanita, strong in voice when it suited an area of confidence. Otherwise, a field of wildflowers around the pools of her eyes. In the wind she would move like pine, not willow. Elegant when pausing, fluent in Spanish and French. Her hands were a constant duet. She wouldn't smile easily, but when she did, she glowed.

"Don't say it, Dr. Quinn. I swear to God I'll walk out of this room right now if you point out I'm expert at locking things up behind six inches of steel just because I'm a banker."

"I may be doomed if I say anything right now, but I have a different thought. Is English your first or preferred language? If not, feel free to slip into Spanish or French. I'll ask your help in translating later."

"English, but thank you for asking. College was good for a few things, languages, business, art, and history, if nothing else. If I start swearing, you'll know it in any language. Now, can we get back to why Che is different? Why can't I just have a brief sexual encounter like I've had before? Why am I starting to care?" Her hands were wringing every drop of water out of an imaginary piece of cloth.

"You speak as if he wants to know you. It may sound ironic, even a contradiction, but I think that's the frightening part for you."

Jason didn't know if she was too full or too empty, but her response was to quietly tell him she was molested as a child, by her mother's boyfriends and a brother. It went on until she was sixteen. Her mother knew it was going on, but lived in a river of booze. Sacrifice was something of a family tradition for the girls, and for what? Instead of being proud when Catalina wanted to go to college, her mother made her feel guilty, then drank up the Sacramento River in a suicide attempt, recovered, had several more attempts, and finally left the world in a cocaine huff. Catalina refined her skills of detachment.

"I guess I got good at being numb." Her last three boyfriends started out seeming strong, even protective, but possession was the price. Kindness came to bother her, and caring was off her list of desired qualities. Shame is a secret prison.

"Now I'm more numb than ever," she said. "Everything goes along fine as long as I'm not a person. Doctor, I'm not ready for this. I think Che is drawn to my complications. Why put my daughter through another failed attachment?"

Jason pictured her staring at the portrait above her bed, sitting on a cedar chest, leaning forward to put on a shoe. Catalina shifted herself in the chair, but couldn't find a place to settle.

"I haven't invited a man over in years. I don't want to be afraid of my own desire. I want to kiss Che like I mean it, even if I don't know what that means."

Her hands were nearly frantic, forming a vice that squeezed out all the air. Each hand took turns covering the other, until they hid under the purse on her lap. She found a tube of lip balm and applied it in a heavy smear.

"You know, Che is tall. I'd have to tilt my head back and go up on my toes to kiss him. I suppose he wants to lean into me and draw me in at the waist. I can see us in a scene, but I can't let it happen. I'm one screwed-up person. He may think I need to take it slow, but really, I'm a glacier."

As she talked, one set of Jason's fingers covered a knee so tightly it hurt. His other fingers floated off the edge of the chair in a dreamy waterfall. In his mind he was at the Bay of Fundy, which he visited thirty years ago. The tide comes in on little waves, but you hardly notice when it's going out. Every six hours it changes direction. You can't go out there safely. It's like quicksand, all the silt.

"What's the deal," Catalina demanded, bringing Jason back to the room. "I've only given Che an outline of my life, and none of it felt real. He must be terribly defective for wanting to know me, don't you think?"

"No, it's never so simple as that. You'll have to ask him more about himself. Make sure you ask about things that matter to you, real questions that a sensitive person will appreciate, not like you're baiting a trap. Listen carefully to everything he says. When you had coffee with him, did you ask about his life?"

"He spoke of a divorce, longer ago than mine. He's got a girl and boy. They travel a lot. We went back and forth in English and Spanish, but like I said, I didn't say anything coherent. I honestly can't remember the rest. He was sad about something, but I was too preoccupied. What if he's just like my dad, who left his whole family on a southbound train? You want to know what's sad, I can't remember my father's face."

She spoke to the vases now, "My mom's boyfriends didn't hesitate to come into my room at night, like it was just the way of the world. I was very good at being still, pretending I wasn't me."

She stroked her hair in a tense quick way, telling Jason of being used and silenced until she ran away at sixteen with a creep no better than the others. The stroking ran deeper when she told of her indifferent mother. The room swirled, or was it was just Catalina's way of twisting her hair between two restless fingers? Jason saw she needed to touch her hair to stay in her own presence, better than biting her lips or scratching.

Jason pushed his own hair off his brow, three times in a row. His hair was blond, three inches long, while hers was thick and dark. The movements of a symphony came to mind. Catalina was a storm cloud in morning, a patient loving mother, conservative banker by day, a work of sculpture for her students, a solo dancer when it suited, a frowning child at night.

"I'll tell you right now," she said, "I don't want my physical presence to evoke a reaction of any kind. Not in anybody. How screwed-up is that?" Jason noticed the conservative long skirt, the high-buttoned blouse. If she was trying to blend into the contours of the chair, it didn't work. If the chair could speak, it would release a chorus of sighs. During a sip of coffee, Jason saw his hands in a line-up, arrested off the street as suspects, exposed behind a one-way mirror.

She didn't like it when his hands made any sudden movement. Even when he put an innocent finger to his cheek, the effect on her was startling. As a child she was hit, subdued, and slapped so many times by her mother, she learned to see it coming. Her mother was drunk by early evening, slept right through the rapes.

Opening the tenth session, Catalina brought her banker self to give the bottom line. "I have to say something before I continue. Dr. Quinn, why do you look at your hands so much? It looks like you're trying to figure out what they're saying? You do a good job of acting like you're calm, but you're not a whole lot more calm than I pretend to be. I thought I was the only one who does that."

Jason took a long look at his uncomfortable hands. The honesty of his fresh look was a comfort to her. It's all she asked—a little validation—and a test of his promise to welcome what she saw.

"You've been talking about brutal hands. Mine are called to witness. They want to show anger at the theft of your childhood, at the men who hurt you, your father who left, your mother slapping you into silence. If I imagine my hands trying to comfort you with touch, it would be intrusive. You had that in your previous therapy, a feeling of betrayal in the end. Your question is impossible. That's what I can say for now."

"Thank you," she said. "I wonder what mine are saying, too. They're rebellious. Even when they're not moving, they're yelling."

In the silence of a redwood forest you can hear the smallest sounds. Jason's hands migrated down the sides of his chair. She saw his struggle: the forced slowness, the hesitation as he matched the pace of his hands with her careful words. When they came to rest, she told of other rips in her childhood.

Not that you could call it childhood, more a collection of images without cohesion: time frames uncertain, confused voices, unexplained irritability, always the damned unwanted tears. It would be an act of distancing to reach for pen and paper. The challenge was to hear it like she said it.

All along, a box of tissues sat on a nearby table. Jason meant them as a courtesy, not a cue. She noticed them a dozen times, but never reached. She had a complicated relationship with the box, and so did he. He imagined what might happen if he gestured toward it during a waterfall. In one version, she says, *thank you, nobody ever did that for me.* In another version she's angry, pacified, as if he's got a problem with her tears right when she needs the river. One day, Jason thought, she'll see a tear of his own, and they wouldn't have to speak of the common purpose of salt.

She settled into the quiet, rocking herself on the verge of oblivion. The motion must have felt safe since she made her chair go side to side, carefully avoiding his eyes.

Without awareness, Jason's hands started looking for symmetry, but it seemed a false goal. He was riveted to the fist in her lap; she came back to it often. Her other hand was pressed flat above her heart, just below her neck. It looked almost like a choke, but that's how things play out after trauma: flipped and inverted, with their own internal logic.

When she talked about rape at twelve, Jason's hands fell to his side in grief. The muscles and bones, bereft of pulse, were barely in the room. Her hands went to her face to cover it, and behind that needed curtain, her voice was as soft as cotton.

"You know, it's like my life is in pastels when I need the primary colors. I want to stop loathing my body. Who the hell do I have to forgive? I've forgiven everyone, myself included. I've read a ton of books, taken self-defense classes, had therapeutic massage, every kind of meditation you can name. I'm still afraid of me."

The deadness of Jason's hands felt complicit. He tried cupping one with the other. At least there was some caretaking then. Catalina wanted him to shake it off, and ride together on a train through the desert, seats facing each other. He could see the approaching world, while she, facing backward, could only see the past. She needed them to change places if he was going to know her any further. All it took was for her to open one hand to the ceiling, the other to the floor. She had no idea of her power.

"My fear is that if I tell Che what I've just told you, he'll be obsessed with the men who hurt me, or worse, he'll smother me with protection. I could see him feeling guilty for wanting sex. Getting close to me can hurt people. I want you to get that, Jason Quinn!"

"If there's a message there for me, we'll be in the storm together. What prompted that thought just now, if you can say?"

"You did the thing I fear. You wanted to hit someone with one hand and comfort me with the other. I saw the twin emotions; don't deny it! It's the same struggle I have with myself. I end up back in the storm, never the clearing sky."

"You said you recently modeled for art students. That comes to my mind just now."

"Not nude; only my face and shoulders. A Bach sonata is usually played in the background. I found I could be an entirely different person if I raised my chin a little, or turned an inch to the left or right. If light found me from a fresh angle, I felt I could start all over. It was seductive. I tried living in fantasies until they started to scare me with fake Hollywood endings. At the end of the pose, I couldn't orient myself anymore."

Jason saw himself in the hallway of her home, in front of a room she did not invite him to know. Surely, there was another room. He felt an urgency to speak, a flash of jealousy, wanting to be in free-fall, wanting to love Catalina from the eyes and arms of Che. The images passed, but she sensed his exquisite confusion. She needed the version of Jason who had no time to think, just his raw response. In a single chance, she might let him be the unfiltered light behind the fallen curtain. Her hands said come and tell.

"Catalina, I have amazing images when we meet: tides, trains, fields of wheat, the scent of lime, a jewelry box hidden in your kitchen. I see intense colors. Always there is white in the end, like a fresh clean sheet. Something in your voice wants me to sleep. But I can't. I see a bench by the river, a beach at low tide. I try to make out a language of speaking underwater."

Both were astonished, especially Catalina.

"You mean I have to risk desire? No! It's too damn frightening. I'd rather be invisible, or hide in the tall weeds. It's safer."

"You can create safety either way, alone or with a person you love."

My dear Dr. Quinn, you have no idea. Let me describe how bad this has become. I have a capacity to go away in my mind. I'm not curious about touch from other people because I'm not even present. People tell me I look lost, even when I think I'm with them. It's like I wake up in a distant town."

"What is it you recognize when you wake?"

"My hands, only my hands. I use them to touch my face or my arms. I use them to induce myself to wake. Sometimes I wake in horror and I need them to calm me down."

"There's a narrative to what fear does. What about the thousand familiar surfaces? A warm cup of tea, the roughness of concrete, a smooth stone, your daughter's hair, a piece of silk, water. These are all touches you can choose."

"Those are not my skin. My skin is a mousetrap."

"I'm reminding you that you're in control of many things. Touch and being touched can come safely as a pair. When was the last time you felt that?"

"Stop being a psychologist. I don't like the psychologist in you. My daughter loves to comb my hair. We take turns. My friends are ok to hug. It's not a prelude to a nightmare. My friend with cancer asked me to touch her breasts before they were removed. I'm going away now, into the portrait above your desk. Please don't follow." She left the room but stayed in the chair.

When she began to breathe normally, after a turn of the tide, Jason said, "Breathe, and find the floor with your feet. What do you see?"

"I see a man bugging the crap out of me. It happens to be you. Oh, I also see a desk, three lamps, a couch and a stupid bookshelf. None of this helps a bit."

"Yes, but you anchored yourself to the solid floor as you said all that. In our early sessions you didn't say you needed to go into the portrait, you just went there, and sometimes stayed or got lost."

"I suppose. Look, my feet are planted. I'm breathing. What's your point?" She uttered something caustic under her breath, a few choice words in French.

"You just widened the zone where you're available to yourself. Tell me, when you practice the cello, how did you come to hold the bow and learn to press the strings on the neck. How did you learn vibrato? You said a note on the cello doesn't have to end. You said a great deal in that sentence."

Catalina caught his meaning—the sensual illustration. The hooded oriole fluttered, and for the moment, didn't fly.

"I experimented. It wasn't about a person. You must know by now, I prefer a cello to a man." They sat in the shadow of the statement, a bit of quicksand there. Finally, she left the session ten minutes early.

On a rainy day a few months later, while talking about her daughter, Catalina saw him reach in his shelf just to touch the dark wood. She saw the soft persuasion and stroked her leather purse without seeming to notice a parallel. It would have been ruined with words. She put an open hand to her cheek, but her face lost all expression. A memory crashed her mind. She told him what it was. He took a breath so he could know. She vowed to never tell the story again. She was drunk at a college party, passed from man to man.

"You know, Dr. Quinn, the whole Central Valley of California was once an inland ocean. I just saw you flooded, then drained. I see that you go away too. It's better than anger or humiliation, isn't it? That's part of my dilemma, how easy it is to go away."

"Yes, I do. I was aware of looking for you in a room I had not visited."

She answered with a smoothing of her skirt. "In the last fifteen years, every time I've had sex, I take an immediate shower and cover up with the thickest robe on earth, even in summer. What's that all about?"

"I think you know," said Jason. She was about to trap him in some hollow explanation. He resisted, and in the stillness that followed, she made a fresh resolve.

"I'm going to tell Che I have feelings for him. But how much should I tell him about my past? I swear I'll never tell him most of the things I'm telling you." She spoke with all the colors. "You know, I'm going to move the portrait of the storm to another room. Where do you think it should go?"

"You will find the right place."

Catalina relaxed her fist while Jason touched the rim of his coffee cup.

"I found the picture of my grandfather, Miguel. It's comforting to tell my daughter about him when I read to her at bedtime. It's odd, when the pages turn, it reminds me of some of our sessions."

Jason thought of the jewelry box he imagined during their first meeting. As he opened it, he caressed his left wrist in the place where he broke it at age twelve. Sometimes the old pain visits. His open hand found the back of his neck, then he touched the cotton sock on his ankle. The mirroring was mysterious. Catalina caressed the arm of her chair as if to say *I know*, then smiled and made another appointment. They parted with a touch of hands. She reached first, as if to seal an agreement, but her touch was not that of a banker, more a dancer, weightless, and their eyes merged like rivers.

Fifty sessions in, Jason had a thought, *if I lean forward, she will frown.* He risked it anyway, wanting his whole body back. Both had reclamation work to do, so he asked about her frown.

"I wasn't aware of that reaction; I was feeling puzzled at what you're going to do next. Habit I suppose. I've been thinking about our first meeting, when I suddenly felt sick, and you brought me some water. You didn't hesitate. It helped me that you let it be simple. Tell me, has anything more important happened in all our work together?"

Jason smiled in a fathomless way. "It would not be for me to say. I've kept that moment close myself."

She started the next session saying she kissed Che on the levee overlooking the Yolo Causeway while a thousand starlings painted the sky in a murmuration. Storm clouds had moved up from Mexico, the remnants of a hurricane.

"My hands were free to touch his face. It was the strangest feeling, easy, like a snowy egret gliding, then landing quietly on the sand. I think we were there on that levee for a whole hour without one word being spoken."

Jason brushed a bit of hair from his forehead and found the day's growth of beard. How like mirth, the birds. It came to him again; she was hushed with a false caress as a child and it turned into a monster's clutch. He brought his left hand to the center of his chest and held it firmly there. Catalina leaned back as far as her chair would go. She'd never gone all the way back before.

"By the way, Dr. Quinn, all this time I've been noticing you're left-handed, like myself. It's a relief, my God, I can't say why. The banker in me notices these things."

By then, Catalina could bring her hands to find the warmth of her sleeveless arms. She'd turned an unused room into a studio, where she practiced cello and tried her hand at oil painting. Her first subject was a field of wheat. The second was an abstract of rice stalks burning after the harvest. The practice has been banned, but she remembered the smoke from her past. It startled him when she swiveled her chair all the way around, like a child at play. It was like an anniversary gift to herself, a whole year in therapy had passed.

"What good is therapy if it can't give you any talent as an artist? I seem to have none. One day I'll try to paint the ocean. I have it in my mind."

It wasn't a question really.

"Speaking of painting, Dr. Quinn, why does it take so long for blue to dry, and for gray to accept the glow of pink in morning?"

When Moon and Sun Were Close

Trevor Jameson looked like an idiot and he probably was, standing too close to the edge of the cliff at Hermaness, on the northern tip of Scotland. If he was trying to make a point with his earnest crouch, left foot forward, hardened to the wind, the point was swept away by the gale blowing off the North Sea as it lashed the Shetland Isle of Unst. The churning sea had called his mind, the rhythmic waves and spew. At twenty-five, it didn't occur to him he was playing the part of the cliffs themselves. It's odd to inhabit a foreground scene with such tenacity, but to only be aware of the distant part. He mustered all the vision he had, ignored the pelting rain, cupped his eyes with cold wet hands, but still couldn't see beyond Muckle Flugga Lighthouse in all the gray densities—not even the dark horizon, where sky and ocean merged.

It's just the kind of thing a young American is compelled to do on a first journey to the isles. In Shetland, with no one else around, he could be a child again. He didn't think to look downwind just fifty yards, or he would have seen a woman. Brae was there, a seeker in the heather, sensible for staying low, cross-legged, unopposed to wind. Her tangled hair and rusty scarf were twins on the way to Norway. Trevor felt a feminine presence even before he spotted her—a gentleness in the tempest, mostly.

These two were as different as a guillemot and a gannet, a skua and a kittiwake, yet similar too, as rocks with kindred shapes. Trevor often wondered if people invent each other out of need. He'd felt a presence like hers many times before, a beautiful turbulence nearby, when rushing on a subway, changing lanes in traffic, pausing in a crowd.

Brae was intimate with the rawness of the land; she could have warned him that in Shetland, perspectives are deceptive, distances compressed, heights impossible, birds too close and quick, or private, as was she.

She saw him dare the wind to either knock him back or admit it couldn't. It never occurred to her to try what felt natural to him. She was more interested in puffins. Look how fast the wings. She watched them dart in and out of view while caressing her long wool skirt and knee-length socks, stopping to throw her hair out of her face as if to shake off something other than the cold.

Trevor caught her motion and matched her presence with her form. He guessed she lived nearby, but wouldn't have guessed her job was gutting fish, or that she hadn't ventured past these islands in all her life so far. The gale seemed irrelevant to her. That alone compelled him. He removed his thoughts from the ocean in front of him, and placed them in the ocean of her.

From distance, he imagined her up close; an angular chin with glowing skin, a bit hard, with spice, very wise, curious in the thin brow lines. All these two had in common was a need to come: a sanctuary for her, a challenge for him.

Portrait of Trevor: full of choice, without a life direction. He'd given himself a summer away from San Francisco to study black-and-white photography. He booked a stay at a croft in Aith near a pretty little voe. Witness the rising plates of treeless land, where shadows are few and anything tall is suspect. It's a place where light stops time in a whimsy.

Portrait of Brae: numbed by routine. The slice and slap of fish on cutting boards gnawing at her dreams. She hadn't set a goal to marry, or walk the streets of Rome. She wasn't sure she would ever need a car. A man she tried to love was cruel when drunk, and she herself had taken to the habit to numb the sting of knowing. She needed more time among the birds—her favorites the pelagic ones that only come to land when it's time to nest.

It occurred to her that the nearby man might have come to the cliffs to end his life. From such a crouch, a man could bolt. Instead, he pulled out a camera. She never wanted a camera; images in her mind were enough. When they saw each other squarely, Trevor offered a nod of recognition, which Brae returned in a measured way. Privately, she wondered what he noticed.

Trevor was keen to the mystery, alert with speculation. She had no car, perhaps a bicycle nearby? Did she come to throw herself off the cliff, or make some grand decision? It's odd; the overlapping suicidal thoughts. In another variation, he fancied her an author, a dancer, come for inspiration. She tried to read his wondering, and he wondered equally about her. That's when they stopped being strangers. He wished he could be with her in heather, when everything around them was chaos.

They left the cliffs separately, without words. There could be a song.

In a week's passage, on the main isle, when moon and sun were close, Trevor was driving on a dirt road and came across a woman walking. He stopped and smiled.

"We meet again, that was quite a day at the cliff."

"I'm Brae," she said, but he already dreamed the name.

"Trevor, the photographer with zero common sense."

She smiled and almost laughed. "I see you found my favorite place, but I doubt you got any good pictures that day. What do you remember?"

"The relentless waves, the wind, and the suddenness of you. I wish I could be like you on the cliff, so peaceful."

"I wasn't peaceful at all. What gave you that impression?"

There was a genuine lilt in her voice, as if she withdrew the question by nuance alone and replaced it with a dance of spins. He offered her a ride. She said she didn't fancy a ride, then paused.

"There's a subterranean cave nearby where water comes in from the sea. I'll show you if you like."

Now the apparition was in his car. He thought of being clever or philosophical, but neither of these matched his honest curiosity. She was matter-of-fact in words, a universe of presence. She saved him and he knew.

"You've heard of the Holes of Scraada, at Eshaness? It's a place where the surge comes in from the sea. Part of the passage is underground. Sometimes you can hear a whistling sound. If you listen carefully, it takes you where it will."

They drove a narrow road, left the car by a fence, and walked to an overlook with surprising familiarity of stride.

"I like it here," said Brae, "you can hear the echo of the ocean, but not the crash of waves. Sometimes I know the language."

Trevor was uneasy, and even shuddered, looking into the abyss.

"This place feels forbidden to me. I think of being lost down there, at the mercy of the tides, with all the voices trapped."

"I'm different I suppose. The water comes and goes, and comes again. It comforts me, like breathing. I listen more than I look. If you're patient, you'll feel the change of tide. I stay for twelve hours sometimes. Come, I have another place in mind."

She took him next to Tingwall. A standing stone is there. They drove to the small stone monolith, which is right next to the road.

"Why is it here?" he turned to Brae. "I can feel it pull me close. It's alone in a field, feels huge, but isn't much taller than myself."

"See," said Brae, "there's a force here, something I can't really show you since you must experience it your own way. It used to be called the Murder Stone. If you committed a terrible crime and could reach it before being caught, it was said you were free from punishment. I think it's stupid. I don't believe it."

"All right, what's your version?" asked Trevor. "This was here before the Iron Age. You get to make your own legend."

"I don't have one. I just know I've been afraid to touch it. I've wanted to. I can't tell which is more ridiculous – the fear or the desire." Trevor sensed permission, then took her hand in his, and asked if she would touch the stone. The air was strangely still.

"Yes, it's time," she found the words, "I would not do this alone," and the tender moment came.

In a minute or an hour, she announced making peace with the stone. She wanted to cry, but couldn't. She wanted to speak of other fears, but barely uttered a sigh.

"Maybe we all murdered someone in a past life," said Trevor, "and hope for forgiveness and sanctuary, or need to run from a huge regret. Maybe the stone takes care of us and calls us back from the edge of cliffs. Look how it fills us now."

Then he touched the stone himself. A power gathered inside him, a mix of centuries upon him, and he faced her eyes to say,

"I would love to photograph you. You astonish me."

A wind came up as he said the words; their eyes went keen and thin.

"I don't like photographs of me. You have an image, don't you, in all the natural ways?"

Trevor said of course he did, and saw the point of her way. He told her he was sad to be leaving for Aberdeen in the morning, that he wished they had more time. Brae seemed to have known it already, the way he rubbed his leg. Or she knew it from the puffins and was radiant all the while—not one to state regrets. He took her back to the road where she appeared, and she left the car and whistled. A sheltie came to her side from behind a stack of peat. In vanishing sweetness, she turned to wave goodbye. Halfway in her turn he took a mental photograph, before her hand could rise.

Tides would know her best. He imagined seeing her smiling on the cliffs when she was eighty-three, always in the heather. Hermaness would keep a place for her, low enough to see the edge, sheltered just a little. He started to drive away, but saw her come again in the mirror of his car. He stopped as she came to say,

"If you make your way to Scalloway, you'll find the image of me you're after."

She was merciful that way.

He was sad at the pretty harbor. Brae seemed to know of his need to go out on the pier where she'd gone many times herself, where piles of ropes were drying on thick wood planks. Beyond, he saw a hundred gulls shadowing fishing boats coming in with the evening sky. Nearer still, he heard the clank of rigging on other boats at rest. She read it in his nature that he'd lean over the ropes with his camera until he nearly fell. In truth, he wanted no release from the sensual ropes, still wet from a pull in the sea. She knew he'd be drawn to the distant part through the call of a foreground scene.

Trevor couldn't see where the ropes started or ended. The dark oval passages, the constant curves, so delicate and close – all of it struck him dumb. These would be their gifts: the touch of a stone for her, the braided ropes for him.

Before venturing to his ferry, Trevor went to a club in the capital city, Lerwick, to hear Peerie Willie Johnson play. The Shetland fiddle is a trance-like fling, where time is disallowed. When he played a version of Margaret's Waltz, the ashes from his cigarette fell to the floor from his serious lips. He paid no attention to the audience, like he was playing to the lost fishermen in all the Shetland Isles. Everyone somehow knew. His long sweet song lifted the midnight air so high that nobody even noticed the falling.

Path of the Ground Birds

Here comes Julian, rounding the bend from his bedroom to the hall, fresh from the hospital and a quick change of clothes. Trauma surgeons aren't supposed to be confused about what to do next, but this is where he stalls. The paths in front of him lead to the front door, atrium, and kitchen. But he's lost, as if in London fog, and forgets the mysteries of trails; how he'll choose one in the mountains because it winds near a stream, or fancy being held, bewitched in a dense forest, or come in need of the sound of bees in an alpine meadow.

He stops on the trail of halls, at the slider leading to the back yard. The yellow hibiscus will bloom any day; the first roses of the year are on the fade, still crimson, and as of yesterday, still sweet. He has no memory of finding his way to the kitchen and opening the refrigerator door, but this is where he next comes into focus, illuminated by the pale blue light from within.

Julian can't tell his own story just now. Too numb. The refrigerator light will have to tell. The tables are turned, the light is soft and kind, like his recent surgery dreams, where the insides of people are telling him about the persons they inhabit; their separate voices speak in casual conversation with his diligent, skillful hands.

While performing surgery, he'll say something like, "I don't believe anesthesia blocks all awareness, do you?" The person is under, but he likes to intuit the whole from just the parts. Yesterday, he found himself whispering, "I'm just visiting," to a section of small intestine.

"I'm going to move you over to take a look around, take care of any problems, then tuck you back in bed personally." Sometimes during a procedure, he hums a bedtime tune using a voice as close to his mothers' as he can summon.

The surgeries of his day were unremarkable in challenge, filed in his mind in an inaccessible vault. Some patients were in critical condition, par for the course in the ER. Here, in the kitchen, urgency has no place. He doesn't move a millimeter, as if competing for stillness with the halibut steaks in the bottom of the freezer. Food is there, but no hand reaches. Cold air spills, seducing and insulating his slight frame, while life goes on around him as usual.

Quails come to the backyard in mornings and evenings, out from under shrubs in neighbor's yards. They take the passage under the fence, where rainwater makes a little riverbed. Every summer he waits for the first visit of the quail parents, scouting the yard for food and safety. A week or so later, the little ones rush from under a bush—in a moving cloud—as many as fourteen. It's his favorite summer moment.

Julian wants the glow of the refrigerator light to stay on him a while longer—in a standoff with other motives. Neither the smoked gouda nor the fresh bowl of tasty olives can shake him from his post.

Any old refrigerator light can see he's not ready to make a move. He might as well be dozing on a beach, listening to rumbling waves. Even if his name were called, it would be from another time, another world, where answering is discouraged, for the sand has spoken—stay.

From the edge of awareness, he hears the familiar sound of his wife's car in the driveway, followed closely by the opening of the garage door, then the jingle of her keys. The gentle sequence drifts upon him, dilating time, while shadows hint at becoming long. But there's plenty of light left in the June day, and Julian's self-awareness returns in the manner of a thin stream of water filling a vacant tub.

His breathing slows and tells of exhaustion. Even so, he notices the edges of perception, the edges of marriage to his naturalist wife, Emily. Usually, he calls her Em, but reserves the intimacy of her full name when they are deep in lust or close to an argument. He can't explain it further.

Em is a naturalist at a nature preserve. She cut her teeth in estuaries of Southern California. Here, in Northern California, she's immersed in an inland medley of songbirds, waterfowl, and raptors along the American River Parkway. She knows which native grasses are being pushed out by invasive species, and laments the water hyacinth, clogging the sloughs in the Sacramento Delta. Em would not have Julian's work in a dozen lifetimes, but knows her piece of riparian woodland as well as he knows the vessels of the heart. She identifies a hundred birds from just their songs; the wrens will often hide.

She comes to the kitchen with a sigh, plops her burdens on the breakfast table, and turns to face her man. At forty-three, Em's recent haircut makes her lengthy presence look French, which he quite likes, but that aside, she enters the kitchen in off-green pants and an ill-fitting blouse with patches of her bland uniform. She's got her hiking boots on, fresh from the preserve, perplexed to see her frozen husband not offer his usual dancing dip or any variation of a greeting kiss. She could have had the thought that he'd be fine with a few minutes of not having to explain himself, but you know how bad timing comes with marriage.

She wanders into the conundrum through a different vein, wondering concretely whether Julian simply doesn't like what he sees in the white box, or if he'll soon make an announcement. Either way, his morass broadens to include her, and she's having none of it. His remoteness bothers her. They've become statues in a modern art museum, inviting speculation.

When motion resumes, their daughter, Kate, enters the kitchen in a brilliant display of ephemeral curiosity, in clear view of Fridgelight (Julian offered this name to the light, as a member of the family who knows everyone intimately by their refrigerator habits). Kate, recently thirteen, has been dropped off after soccer practice by the mother of a teammate. They don't hear her come in, and wonder how long she's been noticing the small drama from the portal to the kitchen. They greet her with poorly-tolerated hugs.

Kate growls that her English assignment is due tomorrow, on the subject of what parents bring home from work. The teacher deliberately made the assignment open-ended and refused to distinguish between physical and emotional matters. Kate offers her protest to the man blocking her way to the fridge, reaches around him for bottled water, announcing her parents should help with her assignment. She says it in a blackmail kind of way, as if they would not presume any higher priority.

Kate is bright; she's mastered perfect timing, asking things in strategic ways. Emily is bright too, mentioning to Kate that self-observation can be a prelude to communicating with others—starting with the interesting trail Kate has dropped off in the last few seconds. There is the jacket she didn't wear, now on the floor of the entry. There is the heavy bag of books hurled on the couch, barely missing grandmother's vase, and the workout bag, dumped in the middle of the family room, with assorted contents spilling out. A soccer ball has rolled into kitchen as if it's been following her all along.

Kate cleverly reminds her mother that her assignment is about parents, not her. She leaves the kitchen with an enviable pivot turn, somewhere between graceful and flippant, to grab a shower before dinner. Em yells down the hallway,

"It's your observations that matter. There is no objective truth, sweet daughter." Their fifteen year old son, Lex, is in Washington D.C. on a field trip. His text message related that national monuments are cool, but he needs money urgently because he was arrested for chewing on a dinosaur bone at the Smithsonian. Can't his own parents feed him? Plus, he's decided to become a taxi driver because they zoom around corners so artfully. He can't imagine a better career.

They miss Lex, but need a break from him too. It's odd to not have his turbulent brilliance in the home. Lex makes things up to counteract the logical sequences he anticipates from Julian and Em, heading off predictable advice, giving himself breathing room. If he and his father are standing at the fridge, and happen to spot the lone piece of chicken at the same time, Lex would choose the moment to announce he's dropped out of school, just to distract his dad. Julian would roll his eyes or otherwise pause, and Lex would grab the chicken leg and run, with a chortle and a victory skip.

Julian speaks to Em, "Kate is smarter than us, you know."

"How so?" asks Em.

"Well, she stays away from metaphor at just the right times. I can't seem to master that. I'm a bit jealous of her nature."

He pours a glass of red wine to warm himself, without a thought as to the other reds of his day. He never gets to know much about the moments leading up to his surgeries; his patients are mostly unconscious or raging in pain. A gulf is widening—between what he provides, and who his patients are. Lately, he's been thinking of fixing machines without knowing their purpose.

Julian's psychotherapist is aware of the gulf. He's certain she enacts a version of it whenever she talks to him while looking at her bookcase. Someday he'll tell her about herself. She'll reach for her teacup, but half the time her hand never makes it to the cup; she'll pull it back and rest it on the edge of her chair, as if the moment is too tender for an actual object to be allowed a role. She is both warm and coolish, depending on the moment: a little like the blue glow of Fridgelight.

Last session, Julian found himself uttering something that shocked him the moment he said it.

"I am a doctor to unconscious people. I wonder how that's playing out in me?"

The same thought re-visits him in the kitchen, with fresh sadness. He thinks he should have mastered these pesky emotions, being a surgeon, zeroing in on the immediate needs of his patients. Emily sees his hand tensing on the door. She's trying to be nice.

Normally, Julian looks forward to Em coming home. She'll tell of her world: the sighting of a sharp-shinned hawk, a prairie falcon, or an otter up on shore. He loves the way she speaks of November, when the tule fog rises from the wetlands in morning, persisting no more than an hour after sunlight.

In summer, he swims the American River while Em walks the trail to meet him downstream. They walk back home on the levee, watching the harriers hunt, the cottontails hide. While not breaking her stride, Em might tell of a child touching an acorn for the first time, or an animal that died only minutes after being born at the preserve. They don't intervene at any birth. He asks about the place of human observation—of sentiment and action. The theme plays between them as a thread of white ink on an all-red canvas.

During a recent walk, Julian kicked a branch out of his way.

"I'm all about blind intervention—for anyone who comes to the hospital. I don't get to distinguish the person from the flesh. Doctors have this oath, you know."

"So do naturalists," said Em. "My work can challenge the instincts of a mother. We have to let things be, but the price is to make rules for human visitors: no dogs (they chase the deer and turkeys), stay on trails, don't go climbing trees, don't plant or remove anything, don't kill a buck, a quail, or catch a frog. It's easy to hate the jerk that cuts down a healthy oak for firewood. The rest is not so easy. Like telling a child not to go where the eyes invite. We get complaints about bee stings and mosquito bites, like we should prevent anything unpleasant."

Julian drifts in the persistence of Fridgelight's glow, quietly fighting a summons from within, to tell Emily of his day. Barely looking up, he finally speaks.

"I had a weird day and I don't know why. Nobody died on the table, but I got to wondering how my patient's lives were going before they got to the ER. I see the quail parents are back in the yard in mornings. I wonder if the little ones have hatched."

Em takes two of her famous long-legged strides to stand closer to her man. She takes a look inside the fascinating recesses of the fridge, then backs off to scan the whole of him, some gray hairs already on his chest, though he's only forty-five. After ten seconds of her own version of a freeze, she says the obvious.

"You're wasting energy. Why don't you decide what you want, then go after it?"

"Just looking," says Julian, with a bit of sharpness. "Can't a man just look?" He tells her that compared to people dying in random accidents or destroying the lives of others, his standing with the door open is not a felony, and feels rather palliative. "I would like, just once, for the pieces of a day to fit like a Dickens novel. Mine never do."

A train pulls away from an unexpected stop in the desert. Julian is on it. He tells her his first patient fractured a femur and other bones in a road rage incident, where the patient caused a five-car wreck. A man in another car, a father of three, died, but Julian didn't learn anything about him. He had a live person in front of him. He didn't get to know which quirks of the day set their fates in motion. The patient on the table would recover, thanks to his intervention. The police were outside the operating room. Blood tests were pending. The patient was cuffed to the bed for when he came out of anesthesia.

There's plenty of black comedy in an operating room. A seasoned nurse speculated, "This is just the kind of thing that happens when you don't let someone merge onto the I-5 freeway. It's either a death sentence or a prison sentence for anyone driving in the hell of California."

Julian quipped, tugging hard on a suture, "No argument, but where is it not hell for this guy?"

Emily softened.

"There are these amazing places in the preserve where cool air collects and gets trapped." She refers to the spot by the elderberry bushes near the river—a place in constant shade. Julian knows it well. The image reminds her of Julian at the Fridge. "I know, we were there just a week ago."

With the door still open, Julian tells her his next patient nearly lost his eye. He sewed up a gash in the man's face after being slashed by his wife, who was on a crack high, wielding a high-heel shoe. His patient was full of profanities, acting all superior, since he'd quit shooting-up a mix of speed and heroin the week before. His wife attacked him because he tried to flush her junk.

Em smacked her head, trying to lighten things up.

"This is why you better not hide my dark chocolate. I have killer heels of my own you know."

Julian thought of a clever comeback, but it didn't reach his lips. He added how the man needed to be strapped down while treated; it was a no-brainer to order a psych consultation. He saw nothing but a revolving door, but felt the intimate madness between people who fight all the time. They can't handle reflection or silence, so they scream or beat each other up. They say shocking, annihilating things, bash each other, and wake up, ready for more, under the same roof.

Now encumbered, Em, places her open hand on Julian's face. She holds it there, which is the best of worlds and the best of languages. He gets the message. She'll measure her response in a language of parallels, telling how people are abandoning animals more and more at the nature center. The list is long: cats and puppies, rabbits, turtles, guinea pigs, chickens and big white rats: all with the rationale that the creature will be all right because of "instincts." She grabs a glass of wine glass for herself.

"What a load of crap," she says. Fridgelight shines on the fact she offers a mirror image of what Julian is saying—about the futility of sewing people up after meth fights. "People don't care about what really happens. They go home smiling and lying to their children. I'm the one to find the remains of the pet rabbit someone got for their kid at Easter. People don't think about hawks and owls, or coyotes."

She tells of pets dying in winter, right under the building that houses exhibits on the wonders of nature.

Julian grows weary at the parallel helplessness, and tries to change the subject.

"I swear the branches of our cherry tree are growing two inches a day in the tender parts just now."

Emily doesn't comment; she looks out the window and notices an empty bird-feeder hanging from a cherry branch. Fridgelight shines on this too.

The same as when Julian reaches for milk from cows, but Em prefers her soymilk. Julian thinks of their debate over the constancy of seeds Emily provides for the birds outside. He's content with seeing which birds come to the summer plants, while Emily offers a never-ending feast. It bothers her if the feeder isn't full. You can't call it guilt, but something close. He's not happy when she cautions him to be motionless in his own backyard just because the hummingbirds are feeding. They're always feeding.

Last summer, it became ludicrous; Julian, grown man and surgeon, complaining to some yellow warblers.

"Why can't you adapt to me for a change? How about a little reciprocity across species?" No answer, no surprise. Mostly the feast is quiet, the evenings long and sweet.

Em vents about a neighbor who thinks it's cute when their cat brings home a dead songbird, probably from their yard.

Julian says, "Some people get off on vicarious killing, or not so vicarious. We're hunters you know, at least the earlier version had to be. Now we've got some choice, and look at the world of choice. More gunshot wounds than ever at the ER this week, and it's not even a full moon."

Most days, he lets tension sink to the bottom of the goldfish pond. Today, he reminds Em of the crawdad massacre last summer at the river? Their children loved them, would even name their favorites. On the way back from the river one evening, they passed another family with a bucket, all smiles, getting ready for a single crawdad meal that wiped out the swimming hole.

Em sighs, "I know, I know. Where's the justice part, where a skunk sprays the cat who killed the warbler, or the cat gets attacked by a possum?" She limits her aggression to the water in a garden hose or a sudden clap of hands.

A raccoon gets their goldfish every few years. It's the reason they don't have koi.

Fridgelight knows all about priorities in the family; one person ignores the cheese but devours the carrots and hummus. Cats kill birds when you let them out, but they get a mouse or rat too, to which there's no protest. "Birds are always out, people should keep their cats inside if they live in a neighborhood."

Julian emerged from the London fog.

"Jays bully the finches. Crows bully the jays. A spider gets a fly. A mantis steals a hummingbird egg." He adds, "Emily, we're not really in opposition. We protect some species, discourage others. We have our favorites. I like amphibians."

Julian likes walking at night to see what everyone has done with their landscapes. It's like the old Thematic Apperception Test in psychology. There's a story in the landscape about who lives there, and a story about what the watcher sees, or misses, or thinks about in the watching.

Em picks up the thread; "Are you talking about surgery, about not knowing the people you're operating on?"

"I suppose I am," Julian responds. "What a pair we are. I'm ethically bound to treat the injured no matter who they are. You're ethically committed to letting nature balance itself with minimal intervention. But what about your war against the star thistle and red sesbania, on and on? You guys rip out those plants with something close to rage. Something's frightening about the word invasive.

Don't get me wrong. I pull weeds too. I take out cancerous tumors. I get the drift."

Again, the proximity to guilt, more like futility, then a lowering of eyes.

"It's anarchy if nobody intervenes. Humans sure as hell weren't native. I suppose the termites will prevail. Weren't they here first? There must be a reason they don't need to evolve much to survive, but what do I know?"

He's pleading to the inside of a refrigerator, suddenly close to tears. Em backs away at his unexpected turn. Julian pulls her in, needing her, reminding her they often share the same outrage, especially when somebody kills a beautiful, non-poisonous king snake simply because it's a snake. Wasn't it only last week he had to pronounce the death of a boy, just fourteen, hit by a stray bullet? Soon, Julian thinks, everyone will claim they're endangered, even surgeons and naturalists, deserving special protection. "Who will provide it? What comes of all this caring?"

"I don't know, but I know we need to eat, and Kate has to get on with her homework." Em mercifully changes the subject. "I counted twenty-three species of birds in the back yard this morning."

Julian thinks to ask her (again) the difference between a titmouse and a bushtit, but lets the question fade. All summer, hummingbirds and dragonflies dart and buzz, making the rounds of Zinnias and Dahlias. A Cooper's hawk makes passes, looking for a mid-air kill.

Last summer a rattlesnake slithered into a vine at neck level on their patio. They caught the juvenile snake in a bucket using a rake, then released it off-trail in the parkway. They are in fine concert, mostly.

Julian finally tells the part he wanted to say when he froze coming down the hall: of a suicide attempt by a young man. He does not get graphic, but tells Em there is extra salt in the tears of a young man who tries to take his life but ends up in an ER with strangers. Em says she's sorry for the young man she'll never know.

Julian says he got to see how grief goes right through the bottom of the earth and returns in the form of tears falling on an untied shoelace. When he was done with the medical part, the best thing he did all day was put his hand on the young man's shoulder, wishing him the other kind of healing. He called for a social worker, and right after that was paged for a hot appendix.

Em says, "Let's not cook. Can we just order out for pizza?"

Julian says, "I can't fix much. Sometimes I want to be one of those candles in a side chapel of an ancient church. That's all I want to be, until I'm finished."Em wants to drift in the Northern Lights, looking down on a still-functioning blue planet. Fridgelight sees there's something stubbornly good about marriage. Julian finally closes the refrigerator door, realizing he hasn't faced Emily until this moment.

Em joins him.

"My day was weird too," but says it with the flatness of frozen tundra. Julian has seen her break pencils on Sudoku puzzles rather than tell what's bothering her. When he stops remembering this quality, she starts telling, leaning heavily against the kitchen counter.

She spent the last portion of her day looking in the dry brush for a fawn reported to be dying in the back acres, likely injured or abandoned shortly after birth. She wondered whether it was unacceptable to the mother. Everyone had a different worrying thought. They normally leave such matters alone, unless there's an extreme reason to intervene, like when an owl was caught in the (human placed) netting near the golf course. Heroic saving is not what they teach or practice. At the nature center, they do not use words like *victim, brutality, exploitation*. Fear is visceral, realistic, necessary.

Julian sees the back of her hand against the dark cabinet door. She doesn't open it. It's a moment equivalent to his own.

The pizza delivery person arrives. Julian takes care of it, returns, and finds her lost. She comes slowly into motion, opening the dishwasher. Dishes are in there, but she's not looking inside.

She speaks, as if to the womb of the universe, in monotone. Emily doesn't know it's a haiku. He feels the mystery of how she filters sadness of her own, offering this about the missing fawn: *We tried to find him, or maybe her, in tall grass, far from any trail.*

"Sweet one, you are sad just now," Julian says, touching the back of her neck. She doesn't know she is this sad. Something in her stirs and settles, with her hand on the cabinet door. At dinner, Em tells Kate about the fawn—saying that several people went searching, and some folks were beginning to trample the undisturbed areas of the preserve, and this became a debate. The search itself carried risks to native plants and burrowing owls and such, plus the tics were out, which also gave them pause.

"My God," shouts Kate, pounding both fists on the table, "you both make life sound impossible to enjoy. Can't it ever be simple? Look, I'm eating a piece of pizza. It tastes good. I made two goals at soccer, got a B on an essay. I refuse to feel deficient. Why can't you be like me?"

Julian responds. "It's complicated when you care about the parts you can't know. By the way, what's in the jar on the bottom shelf of the fridge?"

"It's an experiment," says Kate. "I'm not supposed to tell."

Emily asks, "Is it part of your English assignment, like which parent notices the jar first and asks what's in it? If so, dad wins, but in my defense, he was blocking the refrigerator door for fifteen minutes."

Kate replies, "Sorry. Your question is off limits. I may tell you later and I may not. My teacher says if a parent brings home grease on their shoes from their day as a mechanic, it's the way they tell about it that matters. I'm gonna figure you guys out, I swear."

The wise teacher was after the awareness that refuses to settle—the words, pauses, and trails taken through the house. Julian tells her a brief version of the boy who tried to die but didn't really want to, and how, on the drive home, he was thinking about changing specialties to become a psychoanalyst. Then he'll know much more.

Upon hearing this, Emily slumps and groans, nearly dissolving into her chair, bracing her head with both hands, saying, "Do you realize how long you'll be holding the fridge door open if you do that?"

The moment is so tender, the kitchen light demurs.

They smile and persist. Kate asks, "What am I missing here?" Neither answers. She goes off to write what she's just heard. Fridgelight has been dark for a few minutes now, and tells no more today.

Still in the kitchen, Julian and Emily read a text from Lex.

"Dear family, Washington D.C. is ok, but I'll be moving to French Polynesia soon. This girl I met says the water is so clear and warm, I'll never want to go anywhere else. She's blind and had to touch my face to know me just by feel. I was going to elope with her, except she went home yesterday. Don't worry about my recent addictions; they're too numerous to count. I'll be coming home as planned. My only requirement is you don't try to stop me on my quest. P.S. Pepperoni better be in the fridge. Love, Lex."

Darkness opens the evening primrose; the delicate flowers greet a huge full moon on the horizon, peeking out from behind the redwood tree across the street. Kate's essay is hers to know. She won't show it to her parents. She's not even sure she'll show it to her teacher. All three walk out to see the moon before going to bed.

It ascends above the atmosphere, transforming to white brilliance, casting shadows they don't turn to notice.

Everyone sleeps until the sun resumes narration. The family of quails has come at last, taking the path under the fence, with twelve little ones safely in tow. The humans have learned if they're quiet at the window, the skittish, vigilant quails go right on about their business.

High Noon with Pink Carnations

A conundrum, long-brewing, is the possibility that nobody hated you as a child, not in the dentist's office or anywhere else. It was just the lack of reassurance that made it feel that way, and it didn't help when your mother tried to comfort you by saying that getting your first filling was trivial, since she had root canals without anesthesia, and all you needed was a filling.

Let's say nobody was truly cruel, that even decent parents have unlikely ways of resisting your full becoming. Now you're thirty-five and need to see a dentist, but you think of the first time you were alone in the office, just after your eighth birthday, daring to grow your hair long, beginning to notice your body. Your problem would come when the appointment was over, when you were offered a pink carnation you didn't feel you earned; the kind everyone gets at the dentist, along with a toothbrush and sugar-free candy.

Now you're at the dentist remembering yourself as a child. Just seeing the carnations across the waiting room reminds you of other decisions you need to make: whether to take the new job in the city, or stay and see what happens in the town where you grew up, where everything is familiar.

It was strange having the x-ray machine pointed at your face for the first time, wondering what it would show. The technician was resplendent. She easily saw your secret ways of holding back tears. You put away your hiding tricks because she casually mentioned she cries very easily, like stepping in and out of summer rain. All of it was natural to her, so you wanted to be that way too. She even hummed in a way that made you want to hear her sing. You were safe in her hazel eyes as she put the lead apron on your chest, saying this was for protection. It actually helped—the certain weight of it—and you strangely missed it when it was lifted.

But then she left. The dentist came to numb your gums, declaring you wouldn't feel the rest. But you did. It might have been the first lie you were sure about.

Your mouth was full of cotton, ears murderously trapped by pleasant music. There was an unearthly smell of false mint. Everyone was nice, and your bravery was highly expected. You weren't brave in the slightest, but your feet managed to dance to the sound of the grandfather clock speaking from the hall.

The dentist carelessly left a glaring light in your eyes when she left the room. You pushed it aside and closed your eyes.

Good for you.

Half of your lower lip was numb, and a single drop of spit fell to the clean blue cloth around your neck. You thought of being embarrassed, but instead you started remembering, and could hear your voice inside.

"I miss my real grandpa, our boat rides in mountain lakes. I remember looking over the side of the boat. Grandpa said that whatever I saw there was a snapshot I can look at anytime I want. I saw pillars of light streaking through pure blue water. A drop of water fell from the wooden oar, pushing tiny waves out into the lake. My hair touched the water too, and grandpa smiled because he knew I found something I didn't have to tell about. I want the lead shield back. I want the x-ray person back. I want her hazel eyes on me, and I miss grandpa so bad I can't stop crying in my heart. Why can't I speak?"

No answer came. Visitations are like that. When it was all over, the receptionist reminded you to take a present from the vase. It was high noon with pink carnations. Memory of the next part is filled with prophesy. Maybe you froze, feeling you didn't deserve anything because you cried a little. Maybe you took your carnation with an angry fist, or not at all, or threw it out the car window, or balanced the stem elegantly between two fingers with a mix of defiance and curiosity, keeping it just the right distance from the rest of you while your piercing eyes bargained with places still becoming. Maybe your exquisite eight-year-old arm lifted it to a simple claimed breath.

Yes, sweet child, flowers from dentists are complicated; this one not your favorite color, unexpected in keen fresh spice. The carnation knows nothing of what it gives from the round burgundy vase in the room where everyone waits.

Wombs are like that too. You wonder why you dream of hazel eyes. It was hard losing your grandpa when you were so young. He's in you, you know, not in the grandfather clock. He'll be in you all your life, radiant, present and unfinished. He knew you'd be the best girl, ever, at the dentist. It's like he said; *take two* of the long-stemmed carnations. And you did, wearing your famous half-numb smile.

The Couple that May Still Live on Maple Street

A cherry tree receives me at the end of a day of psychotherapy, in the privacy of my yard. The wood is the softest I have known. I've always thought it's the shade of the tree, the June shade stretching toward the fence, which offers the sweetest welcome. Never judging, always predictable, its leaves are the shape of teardrops. Shade is the master of stretches, obedient to the sun. If I stand in the dappled light, I see shadows within shadows. I've just left a session with a married couple. They turned on each other, steel-eyed, wringing the last sarcasm out of the moment, until they flat-out glared through their own spit. My office couch was not quite dark enough to suit a re-creation. Divorce was in the air.

For a moment while I was with them, I wanted to be the man in the ice-cream truck going around the neighborhood making children happy. I also find refuge in the macro-world; there are beautiful patterns in my cabinet door that I count among my friends. I needed them today, because witnessing the end of a twenty-year marriage meant visiting a unique silence, where light is not allowed. It always feels like winter, even if it's best for both.

There were endless claims of victimhood, but no apology that mattered.

"I was an idiot to marry you," the wife said, baiting the man she once poured herself into. If she was expecting him to agree, it wasn't going to happen. Really, the early sessions were leading here all along.

"It's the other way around," the husband answered, in a flippant, dismissive way.

"Don't you ever get tired of acting, because you used me from the start."

For four months, they'd been talking about how good it was in the early years, but now the venom flowed. Therapy had been moving too smoothly. Something didn't ring authentic. The permanent lean of a cypress tree came to mind, the way they take the constant wind and are sculpted, beautiful in their ways, persistent I suppose, but lower and lower to the ground. There would be no victim or saint – just two people lost in want, full of enmity, swimming against denial. After all the digging in, they couldn't reflect, grieve, or show minimal concern for the other. Smug indifference prevailed. Don't even read this if you've been there. Both had claimed high ground in the suffering. Was it complicated? Yes and no.

I couldn't even find a dirt road to them. They wouldn't tolerate me trying to find them in the ghost of a shared moment. A storm was on the horizon. They didn't want a mediator, therapist, minister, priest or sage. No rabbi, friend, or lawyer. It was more like they sought a portal, but a mirror is what they found.

Here's the crunch-time image: they folded their arms over the upper chest while crossing their legs in opposite directions. But it wasn't quite equivalent; there was a slight asymmetry in avoidance. I wondered if they did this when nobody was around. She said yes, he said no. Each stared at a different object in the room.

The shade of the cherry tree might have advised me differently, but I didn't offer a predictable response. I said, "Some couples find their passion in arguing until it becomes senseless and nobody's listening." They needed to be in it together.

Gone was the baiting manner of last session, when the wife asked, "Did you remember you agreed to pick up the dry cleaning like you promised, or did you forget as usual?"

Gone was the raise of the ante; "I'm sure the doctor has better things for us to talk about than the dry cleaning," delivered with sharpened teeth.

So the husband found a walnut bookend to be his studied companion, while she scowled at an empty vase. Both of them noticed my tall cabinet, like it might open by itself, and show them something they needed or missed. I would have been glad to show them the contents: books, photos, favorite quotes pasted to the shelves. Neither would ask what's in there, but couldn't take their eyes off the closed doors.

Then the wife turned to me, and said, "Can you believe his tone?" And before I could collect a response, the husband said, "I'm done, just pay the man. I want a divorce." She said, "No problem, you sanctimonious prick. But you have the goddamned checkbook, so you pay him."

I remember my left shoe being most compelling object in the room, but I managed to put my hand up like a stop sign to say it was high time they deviated from their tightly scripted cross-complaints.

"In a different light, this could be your finest cha-cha; your one-upmanship is top drawer. Let's agree that divorce is not always a failure. Plus, I've seen good things come from a separation." I said it calmly, which kind of shocked them. I wasn't finished.

"Think carefully about what you need to say to each other right now. You are both in a great deal of pain. Let's take a moment."

Well, neither of them got up or resumed their rant. Nor did they take back what they said. Neither looked in my direction or scanned the cabinet doors. The eyes went low but there weren't any tears. The next five minutes were filled with a particular kind of silence: a three-person silence. Strange things happen in this place. They might find each other amid the ashes. I've seen it a hundred times—an overture of repair rising from a glimpse of the abyss. Something like,

"Nothing I do will please you. Let's say I picked up the dry cleaning and got you a pretty blouse too. You would find a way to undo the kindness and remind me I should know you hate that style, or tell me it's too little, too late. You'd make it another example of victimhood."

Then the other might say, "I wouldn't, I swear. You aren't being honest about how miserable you've become." Good things can come from talking about the self to the other.

But today, with this couple, the wife held up two fingers, indicating the number of years since they had sex, or even talked about it. The husband rolled his eyes, always a bad sign, saying he wasn't the one who gave up, that he grew tired of the report cards she gave. A circle is a circle. I wasn't there to see the dance, but it was close to the steps they showed.

I cautioned them about saying things with intent to hurt each other further, as they've mastered this numbing art and can freely visit another room in the gallery of life. Either or both could get on with who they want to become. Maybe a magician would have had a better perspective. Who knows? Years later, they might agree this was the lousiest year of a very decent marriage, or a pivotal session where they used the silence for something other than to drown themselves.

Now I'm home, talking to a cherry tree at the end of the day, in the shade of another language. Wait! What do I mean by *shade of another language?* Just a thought about meanings, when words are not enough. Words can be like balloons lifting from a carnival crowd. Meaning arrives from within.

A scrub jay chases the doves from the feeder. I've read that mourning doves mate for life. These doves are up in the tree, looking down. I've seen their tattered nest, so different than the tidy cup of hummingbirds. Where do I file the day? My pager is ringing. One of the pair I saw today might be calling right now for another appointment, or to say they're done keeping a huge secret that explains everything, or the silence really got to them, or they're never coming back, and thank you for the effort. I won't know any more today. The shade of the cherry tree might know, but it's merged right into the night.

A Son in Tennessee

As a young man visiting Scotland, I was drawn to Roman walls. I'd come on gray mornings where no trees grew and heather was months from blooming. One way led past lakes, the other to hills in mist. I thought of ancient soldiers sloshing through the centuries in peat so rich you could burn the earth itself for warmth. I was lost in wars I never fought, in all their killing causes. I'd sit on walls until sun appeared or sky surrendered rain.

I'm older now, a therapist in a warm room, with another kind of cold. A man asked to see me because he couldn't stop lying, but first he lied, calling to say my bad directions left him stranded in traffic. But there he was, talking to me on his cell phone from the parking lot, testing me for blame. I saw him from a window.

I consulted my office paintings of autumn paths, oak trees, a ship on a yellow river. When he opened my office door, he announced his larger problem.

"I can't feel anything real. There's a storm inside my head."

I wondered if mist between men will ever lift. But this man found my door, and more; he told of dreams where walls have brilliant murals but he couldn't come up close because a monster blocked his way.

Then he said, "I made that up. I have no dream for you. That's how easily I lie."

"The hell you did," I said to him, "there's truth in the lies you choose. And what of childhood?"

He gave version one thousand of the kid who never got the shiny red bike promised by the vicious step-dad. He heard his birth father remarried, has a son in Tennessee. His mother drank herself to death—slapped his face plenty—now he lies to decent women if they touch the slightest scar.

I was surprised when he came again.

"Sorry for last time," he said, "I'm sorting through the trash."

I nodded to a distant star. Then he changed his story about who was vicious when he was a child, and who died from drink. There was never a son in Tennessee.

"Would you care any different if I'm gay or want to be a she?"

I deferred to the Roman wall in a solemn invitation.

"I've been away to war," he said, looking out the window.

"War, you say?" I had to ask, since wars are not the same.

We shivered this way in long slack tides, for weeks and months and years, until someone outside was raving, racing toward us down the hall, clawing colors off the walls. His monster, I presumed.

"This always happens," he said.

"Then it's time we see a face," I replied.

I opened the door to an empty hall—no beast that we could see. The air was mean, the light obscene, like a fire needing fuel. He said I wouldn't believe his truth after all the lies he's told.

"You might be surprised at what men carry, at what you're ready to say."

Then he looked at my office painting of the ship on the yellow river.

"Where's that ship headed, I need to know—the one in your painting there?"

"You're welcome to come and see for yourself."

He left his chair to take a look, while I, on watch, stood by. He studied it intensely while I thought of Roman walls.

"Doctor, you first. Please."

"To me, the ship is beautiful in its distant invitation. There's a layered mystery in there, plus I love the backlit sky. Sometimes I think it's sunrise, but it could be an evening glow. It's never been clear to me if the ship is waiting for a tide, or about to bear a load."

"What is it anyway, about men and ships and tides?"

"Speak your truth. It's time you hear the person who cares is you."

"Ships are built for the open sea; this one's going to leave the river after repairs from a vicious storm. I'm wondering about the smaller boat—the one in the foreground shade. I can't make out if there's just one person in the boat, or two."

Another boat? What kind of horseshit is this? I thought. I had to come close to see for myself. I felt a shiver then, for I'd seen the print five hundred times, but missed what he saw first.

Variations on a Ruse

Ralph and Stella Murphy wanted a child, but they didn't know why. They weren't happy to begin with, so a baby wasn't going to be a solution. Their neighbors grew tired of their arguments, buckets of vulgarities sailing over suburban fences, filled with cross-complaints and futile pleas, followed by the dangerous kind of silence. Ralph's friend and fellow plumber, Ernesto, likened them to the gurgling and hissing of old steam radiators, just before they blew.

Last week when he visited, he came upon the scene of Ralph and Stella walking down their driveway, holding two sides of a box they were throwing out, too heavy for either to lift alone. It was filled with Stella's collection of pottery. Every piece had been methodically broken and she wouldn't say why. She lined them up in in her backyard, named them, and crushed them with rocks she brought from the riverbed. She loved the rocks, the layers and patterns, the millions of years in her mind. She loved the smooth surfaces that call from under the freezing water in winter, witnessed by the great gray sky. When they're wet, you can see their complexity, their beautiful striations. That's when she chooses them—not when they're dry and pale in the blistering heat of summer. In summer, she loves them only at midnight, when they're warm but no longer hot. She places one against her cheek, closes her eyes, and thinks of their endurance.

"Ralph," said Ernesto, "you and Stella are held together by a some weird glue of resentment, but you can't be pried apart with a crowbar. I'll never figure that out. Why can't you make life simple like me? I was one of seven children born into poverty. I learned a trade, married a sweet gal just out of high school. I really don't want to fight with anyone, especially my wife. At least we'll always have work as plumbers. Hell, I make as much money as my dentist, and he's miserable. Between fillings, I give him relationship advice. I actually think he's suicidal."

"I guess you don't have a wife that reminds you to be miserable like mine."

"No, I suppose not, but why do you stay together? Forget it, don't answer that. Look at me, a fine example of a man who has all he needs, except for a beer in this outstretched hand."

Stella's last pregnancy test was negative, like all the others, and she was flat out done being tearful. The box they threw out also contained their wishes, for a home they could afford, better jobs, a forward look, a reliable car, as if these might stop their bickering and malaise. Ralph pulled Ernesto aside to fill him in on what he was witnessing.

"A baby, hell yeah it would be nice, but it'll happen if it happens. Our doctor said there's no obvious medical problem for either of us, and he thought we could use some counseling before Stella and I start destroying each other, like counseling might give my sperm a better aim, her eggs a sure welcome. We tried in-vitro fertilization for 12K a pop, and used up her parents savings. Then we went to this class on infertility, how it puts ridiculous stress on a relationship, as if we didn't already know. I swear I would have shot myself if I had a gun right then, sitting in a room with strangers, waiting for our turn to talk. I couldn't do it, so I made up a story about having the stomach flu and we left. Lying came easier after that. But wait till you hear about our game."

Ernesto, who had two boys in soccer, was looking mighty glum, unsure of what to say. Having children was the easy part for him. Ralph added, "It's ok, we decided on a different kind of therapy. I don't know what gives your marriage spice, but Stella and I decided to go to therapists using false names, playing by a simple rule: we make up fake problems and stay in role the whole hour, no matter how weird the script plays out. It's almost the same as having real problems, but we're bored with the ones we have. You should try, maybe just between yourselves for starters. Like going to a restaurant and pretending to be other people than you are. I think it's good for Stella, I'm doing it for her, until a child comes along."

Ernesto replied, "Shit man, it sounds like a lot of work. You're paying for this? Why don't you just go camping in the snow without a jacket? I know, you can try going out fishing when a hurricane is coming in?" Ernesto was the best kind of friend. Non-judgmental.

"Tried that, tried everything we could think of. No juice. All we did was argue."

Stella overheard the last part and chimed in, wanting a little credit for her part in the ruse.

"Get it, the therapist probes our histories and complaints. I'm actually better than Ralph at giving false leads and making up things on the spot. I use innuendo. I want you to know, I'm very, very good."

Ralph agreed, saying, "I'm a pretty decent actor too. Not bad for a plumber, eh?"

When Ralph went to use the restroom, she spilled her secret to Ernesto.

"I'm doing it all for him, you know. Ralph's been so depressed."

Ernesto left in a newly-leased Toyota, shaking his head all the way home to Fairfield. He missed the recession because he didn't own property then, but the Murphy's were hit like a sucker punch in Vacaville, halfway between San Francisco and Sacramento. Their rental home is so close to the I-80 freeway they have to listen to constant traffic, a rumble of waves—ugly waves of meaningless noise. For five years they tried to conceive a child, just not in recent months. After Ernesto went home, the Murphys plotted.

"What's our next story going to be?" Stella yelled from the kitchen to Ralph, who was lounging on the couch, flipping through nine hundred TV channels with the sound off.

"Come on honey, I'm tired of choosing. You always do this. You wait until I'm totally chilled out then ask me which story we'll cook up for the next marriage counselor. We'll defeat them all, you know. We're good at this, don't forget we're a team. Nobody does what we do, it's groundbreaking."

Ralph was tired of telling how he lost his retirement account because he listened to his stockbroker, who in turn listened to fraudulent accountants. Their realtor told them, *get in while it's hot*, and their banker said *sure, no problem*, to a 500K loan when they were making 50K between them. Bankers didn't go to jail for ruining millions of lives, but their neighbor's son, a gentle dreamer of a lad, went to jail for two ounces of marijuana. Stella peered out the kitchen window, recalling what she told her confused parents.

"The bank gave us a loan, and we bought a gigantic home, which lost half of its value in one year. We had to declare bankruptcy and give back the new furniture since we bought everything on a credit card. Our truck was re-possessed. We've decided to lay low for a while, you know, ride this thing out."

She didn't want to worry her parents further. What she didn't tell them was the tide kept going out. Stella lost the lease on her nail salon and now works out of the rental home, telling stories of woe to her few remaining clients. She recalled the night, a few months ago, when Ralph shared his inspiration.

"If we're going to see a goddamned marriage therapist, we're going to do it our way." Stella refined the agreement. Expressing honest emotions was against the rules of the therapy game, but the larger violation was receiving vicarious therapy. They didn't want therapy; they wanted a challenge, to be in the drivers seat for a change. It occurred to Stella that a troubled marriage in America is a walk in the park, but faking one might take some effort.

In their first encounter, Ralph took the name Luigi, who was having an affair with a college escort. Stella inhabited Alice, a workaholic wife who pretended she didn't know what was going on. Stella fumbled her opening lines, but went on to play a credible woman who just discovered being betrayed.

Even a novice therapist notices a deliberate pinch of a knee, a roll of the eyes in silence, leading to any number of meanings. Stella played the young therapist like a fiddle, but was bored with how easy it was. Ralph came to an instant conclusion.

"It's easy to fake out therapists. They assume at least one person in a couple is coming for help, even if the other stays shrouded in a cloud of skepticism. Outright acting is unexpected. Still, we have to be more imaginative."

In real life, Stella was flighty, goofy cute, impatient, and sarcastic. It bothered her from the start that she couldn't erase herself by being Alice. Ralph underestimated the task of being Luigi, wondering, in the hours before dawn, why he chose the scenario he did. After all, he was no longer the Romeo he was at first. He didn't know it, but Stella was actually the one thinking about sex with others, feeling Ralph didn't want sex with her anymore, that it was too much a chore, the baby-making business. She came to regret the lightweight acting assignment she'd given herself; too constricting for a woman of her talents. The game was already falling apart.

To break out of the rut, she came to the next session with a pop psychology story, implying she had a Dissociative Disorder (she'd done her reading) and was unable to remember the first therapy session, along with ninety-seven percent of her childhood. She reported vague scenes of being ritually molested by everyone on the block, and said she was routinely left alone at the age of three with curtains drawn when her parents went off to bars. That's what a relative told her. She couldn't recall what she did for self-soothing, but certainly didn't think any of that was relevant, flipping her hair just a little to mimic *la belle indifférence.*

Some therapists would think they hit the jackpot and write up the case for an academic journal. And you know, the damn thing might just make it to print. Therapists never claim to be investigators, so when a guy says he suffers from road rage after a tour in Afghanistan, there won't be a request to prove he was in the army. It takes a while in therapy before stories gather in a credible way, but the Murphy's were more interested in entertainment. Besides, sometimes an expert will say, *facts just don't matter, it's what you feel that's important.* Other experts will shake their heads and say, *where do we draw the line?*

In spite of missteps, the Murphy's were quite pleased with their next two sessions. They'd laugh the devil's laugh all the way home, and have pretty good sex using their fake names to keep the chemistry going, before deciding on new characters to inhabit.

Stella had more fun playing screamers than any other role. She realized she might have overdone it when she threw herself on the floor of the office as Alice, begging Luigi to come back, clutching his leg, crying.

"I'll come back when I feel you really need me," said Ralph, choking on his words. "It's ok," said the confused therapist, "we'll work through this. I'd like to see you a bit more often." It wasn't to be. Ralph and Stella had run out of steam. Stella wanted to ask if he did in fact need her, but that would have been against the rules.

They wouldn't admit it, but they almost met their match with Dr. Theodore Green. He earned the nickname Dr. Deadpan because he took their presentation so much in stride they had to include wacky details just to get a rise from him. Ralph, as Virgil Chandler from Arizona, finally leaned forward to say he could prove he was reincarnated from Genghis Kahn, but his boss still won't give him a raise and now he's thinking of killing him. The doctor said it wasn't so unusual to identify with powerful figures from the past, especially ruthless people who crushed their opponents. After all, the mind can cook up solutions that can be quite elaborate and satisfying. Lots of people get a raw deal and feel stuck in jobs they hate. Did he actually plan to kill his boss or was it just a thought? Did he hear voices, or just believe he had a special link to Genghis?

Ralph grumbled, didn't try to answer at first. Then he realized he didn't want Dr. Green to alert the police, so he backed down. "I'm not going to kill the asshole. But I'm telling you right now, Dr. Green, I wouldn't be sad if that man has a horrible end."

Stella felt it was time to rescue him, playing Dixie, an unsuccessful realtor. But she didn't really think it through. She started sobbing on the couch, searching for an opening remark that just wasn't coming. Ralph saw she wasn't ready to jump in, and decided it was time for plan B; to say that his more immediate problem was recurrent nightmares of George Bush talking about weapons of mass destruction. The therapist assumed it was an example of traumatic fixation or the vicarious type of PTSD. Ralph had Dr. Green going at that point, and for icing on the cake, Ralph made up a story that their son came back after serving in Iraq and now lives in emotional poverty, unable to laugh or love. They felt they'd lost him.

Trouble was, Ralph always wanted a son in real life, which only Stella knew. Back in the old days, Ralph was sure he fathered a son he wasn't allowed to meet. His girlfriend left him in the middle of the night with a note saying he'd never get to meet the son she was carrying, on account of him being such a jerk. Ralph never knew if she was just torturing him out of spite, or telling the truth, which was another kind of torture. It bothered him unaccountably whenever he had to do any kind of plumbing job that required reverse threading. His tears were like a leaking faucet—one he couldn't fix. The mention of a son just slipped itself into the therapy session. The story was suddenly so sad, everyone in the room found tears, and some were genuine. Stella fumed, as Ralph was breaking their rule by alluding to something real. It was going to get ugly.

Dr. Green suggested that a little grief work, emotion-focused therapy, and community support ought to get them back in the saddle. He asked what the VA system was doing for the son? Virgil choked up for real, and Stella knew Ralph was tumbling right out of his disguise.

Everything was spinning far too close to home. Virgil needed a break from his script, so he prompted Dixie into action by outing her on a different topic. Suddenly, it was dirty fighting, even for the Murphy's.

"Doctor, there's another thing. Dixie, sweetheart, I didn't want to bring this up, I swear, but you're not yourself ever since you started selling Mary Kay products. I know you love it, but you're so distant from me now. I can't prove it, but I fear this outfit tries to take over a persons' life. It's certainly taken over yours."

Dixie was dumbfounded, suddenly wanting Ralph to drown in his mention of a son. It was not a safe topic. She really did want a child. Ralph was pushing fifty. Stella, at forty-two, was in crunch time. On their living room table were pamphlets on adoption, still unopened.

"Mary Kay products are decent. That's more than I can say for you," she pouted, crossing her arms with her fingernails jabbing her upper arms. Ralph had done a little theatre in community college. He was pretty good as George in *Who's Afraid of Virginia Woolf*, but the role actually frightened him, the dripping sarcasm didn't fit back then. He also figured there's more security in plumbing than acting.

During the drive home, Ralph tried to blow the session off, turning on the radio, but Stella shut it off in a way that let him know she wasn't going to drop it. He (sort of) apologized, and told her he'd be more careful in the future, also more creative. He already had some ideas in mind to bounce off her; a gambling problem here, a lurid sexual habit there.

Stella wasn't buying the distraction and pounded the dashboard like a drunken hysteric. Except she wasn't acting. She didn't forget what had happened, and simmered in her special way, plotting her next move as Dixie. She got even in the next session, telling the therapist she saw photos on Virgil's cell phone from a transgendered man, with a caption, "Want some of this, big boy?"

"Don't I have all the goodies you need?" Dixie cried, really turned on the waterworks until she was sure the therapist looked on with compassion. Virgil didn't skip a beat, and said his friend Ernesto sent the photo to him as a joke. In truth, Ralph and Stella were getting a little tired of Dr. Green, who didn't budge from insisting they were working through something vital, even if they didn't know what it was. On the way home from that particular session, Ralph fancied Dr. Green as a pathetic man, and was sure he was a *Wheel of Fortune* addict, eating frozen dinners while his mummified wife was posed in a back bedroom with a teacup in her hand. Stella had Dr. Green as a decent man who was horribly lonely, but conceded Ralph had it partly correct. She said it wasn't Dr. Green's wife who was mummified, it was his dead dog that he came home to pet for hours at a time. Ralph stood his ground.

"Nobody can be like Dr. Green and not be a killer. Nobody." He called Dr. Green from his cell phone to end further sessions, saying he just landed a dream job in Las Vegas, and thanks for all the help.

The next therapist was a young gal just out of grad school. Dr. Martingale asked the couple to make lists of their favorite expressions of love. Stella (as Grace this time) ate it up. Among the acts of devotion she wanted from Conrad (Ralph with a southern drawl) were for him to bring her roses thirty days in a row, with a fresh love poem every time, handwritten of course. Conrad was a minister with an internet porn addiction, and was ready to do anything she asked. He confessed to going to strippers too. What could possibly be next? They couldn't risk therapy in their own small town of Dixon, which is why they drove to Vacaville for the meetings.

Dr. Martingale noted all this calmly on a yellow pad and offered a book to Conrad, who pretended he was relieved to no end that he wasn't the sickest man in the sight of God. He claimed to be cured in three sessions, and Grace was the happiest woman in all the land.

On the way home, they detoured to a sex store in Sacramento and spent two hundred dollars on toys. It was a riot for the Murphys. "Who knows," Ralph said later in bed, "maybe all this acting will be good for our real marriage." Stella upped the ante as she always did. "You choose the next therapist, and make it a good one this time, not Dr. Deadpan or another newbie, or maybe your little preacher's wife won't be so nice at bedtime anymore."

"All right, all right, how about this one: Oliver Faulkner, great literary name, let's give him a try."

At sixty-five, Dr. Faulkner had a habit of looking at his aging hands before sessions. As the veins and bones were more revealed each year, his peace was somehow there. A colleague told him he had a seasoned view of the human psyche, and his students knew him for his relentless search for hidden stories.

When Dr. Faulkner came out to his waiting room to welcome his new couple, there sat Jed and Florence Harding. Handshakes all around. They filled out his intake form and Jed announced, all proud, as if the doctor should know, he was past president of a Rotary Club in Tennessee, and did Dr. Faulkner belong to the local?

"I'm saving a lot of things for retirement," said Faulkner. "I've got a 1958 MGA I'd like to restore, some travel in mind—then, who knows?"

Florence looked Dr. Faulkner in the eyes with genuine authenticity, saying she'd heard he was a good therapist from her friend Eunice, who heard it from someone in their RV club.

Dr. Faulkner nodded to the effect it was nice to have an endorsement, but his wheels were already spinning. Something was too scripted about these two. Why the bother, why the folksy comments. They weren't at a crab feed for little league. One of his activities was to consult to new therapists in training. Not so long ago, Dr. Martingale brought a case for supervision, telling of a few bizarre sessions with a couple named Grace and Conrad (the wayward minister and his pretty wife Dixie), saying she found it hard to believe Conrad when he told her she was extremely helpful and he was eternally grateful. She didn't feel she did jack shit for the couple. Dr. Faulkner agreed.

"You're right to be skeptical. I think they're terrified. They're dancing too close to something that's depleted them, and they're the last to see it. Probably the husband promised the wife he'd see a therapist, as long as they didn't talk about a certain problem. I see it all the time. What else did you notice?"

"The woman looked at me with a flash of desperation, like she was trapped in a role and couldn't get out. It was weird. She said she wanted roses and poems, but I cringed, like I was watching a TV show from the 1950's. I took a harder look at her, and I swear there was a part of her that actually wanted roses once in a while, maybe not poems, but something was there. I remember making room for her to respond to him, and she started to actually appreciate that. He went on and on about himself. Derivative talk. I asked him to back off from his story and say something about why he needed her in his life. He couldn't, he got all flustered, like the thought never occurred to him. Then he said something about a garden they used to have, but couldn't really say more. They left after only three sessions, thanking me as if they were all better. I blew the case, jumping into dumb suggestions before allowing a deepening."

"No you didn't. Don't be too hard on yourself. I've been doing this for decades and I'm still dumbfounded by the difference between a complaint and a plot. You have to let go of what you think will help and follow your intuition. I think this couple is rather desperate, that they've colluded in some unusual way. Lets say the husband wants sex wearing a teddy bear costume. It won't come out in the first session. Deception is interesting from every angle. Things will get revealed if they stay. For sure, you'll be offered a role. Don't take the bait to accept the first one they offer."

"Role? Like healer, savior, obstructionist, sycophant, detective, bad mom, maybe a sponge?"

"You can count on it."

Faulkner amused himself at the realization the two people in front of him were the ones his trainee was describing. Now it was his turn to see what they were up to. He gave them each a fatherly stare, and vowed to wait them out. It worked, a simple thing like that. The Harding's began to unravel, the accents faded, along with the folksy diversions. As skilled as they were, the bloom was off the rose.

The Harding's no more than sat down before going at it for real. Even Faulkner was surprised. They didn't try to induce him in a set-up, as cons will often do. A while back, another client started limping, unconvincingly, saying, "Oh by the way, I have a few disability forms for you to fill out." It wasn't like that at all.

In the twist of a melon vine, Jed and Flo weren't acting anymore and Faulkner had to press the reset button in his mind. Something primitive disturbed him, sending chills down his arms and legs. When therapists are rattled they ask for context, breathing room, perhaps a bit of history. They hardly ever say, "I'm flat out confused, help me out here."

"Sure," said Flo, who was by far the better keeper of history and context. Jed threw his hands in the air and glared at the squares in the ceiling.

"We've had a lot of deaths of family members, my mother is fading with Alzheimer's, we spent all their money, I had breast cancer ten years ago, both of us drink too much, we're sarcastic, we've had two miscarriages, identity theft, and a bankruptcy. You know, typical stuff."

She listed them again, slowly, like a dirge, so her husband could see she wasn't kidding around anymore. When Jed tried to change the subject, she threw the list back in his face. They tried the simplicity of blame, but the path led to poison oak.

Dr. Faulkner decided to speak to the space between them. "These are oceanic challenges to your marriage. If you lived through all these things without talking to each other, the healing from it can't be a shared reality. It might even seem futile, making you each feel more alone than ever. Jed, what would you add here, the losses and stresses on your end?"

Ralph saw his wife had broken the rule and he hated her for it. Payback time. Full circle. Everything she said was true, but he still found an arrow in his quiver and handed it to himself as Jed.

"For starters, I notice my darling wife didn't mention she has a compulsive gambling problem and we're barely able to afford this appointment. I don't see us getting back on our feet financially, and she blames me but she's the one who needed the big house we couldn't afford."

Jed rose further from the ashes, trying to resume the game with an accusation that his wife had poisoned his beloved homing pigeons.

"You did it. Tell the truth. Nobody hated them except you!"

But Stella no longer wanted to play. She turned a little red and turned to Dr. Faulkner like she was the sweetest flower in a vase, but was doomed to facing the wall.

"I can't do this anymore."

"Do what? What's going on here?" Dr. Faulkner was very patient.

"We had an agreement, a stupid game with false identities."

Jed interrupted. "Don't listen to her. She broke the rule, not me. Here's the deal. We can't have a baby in the natural way."

Stella planted a bomb, screaming, "OK, now it's time for you to tell the truth. You didn't even shed a tear when I went in for the miscarriages. You acted like it was an oil change for our car. You're not all in."

"What?" yelled Ralph, "I didn't bring all this on myself. I work every day while you work two hours a day and won't even look for an outside job. You've been drifting through the last five years on Xanax and booze, now you say I'm the problem."

"You're missing the fact you make me miserable, asshole. I've felt alone for a long, long time."

"I want a baby too. I wasn't sure before, but now I am. I'm ready to adopt."

"Like hell you're ready. Just last night you said the opposite."

"OK, OK, I just wanted you to be realistic. Couples end up fighting for the right pre-school opening, then they interview t-ball coaches, have to figure out carpools and playgroups and daycare all before the age of five? Then a teacher says your child has some terrible learning problem because we drink the local water and before you know it your kid has five pathological labels. What will we tell our kid in gridlock traffic, late for a swim meet, eating fast food in the car, in debt up to our eyeballs, about why we care about anything?"

Stella was silent, but wickedly cruel. She stood up, as if on stage, and turned toward her broiling husband. "I just want a child. I want to love a child, and for us to love a child. We'll figure it out along the way. I'm happy to adopt. You only mention the horrible parts. We used to laugh. We can make it work."

A mockingbird called from outside the office, imitating a jay. Dr. Faulkner was left in the dust while they had it out, halfway out the door.

"One last thing, Ralph. I'm pregnant. It's a boy. Since we're calling this therapy, you should know I made a mistake and had sex with a guy I met at the store. It was only one time, I swear. I'm sorry. I was mad at you, real mad, and you couldn't be bothered to look up from the TV. I don't even know the man's name. But the child can be ours if you want. I want a divorce if you don't. That's the thing I want from you, an agreement to be a family. One fucking little recession and you fall apart, whining about it constantly. Are we in this together or not?"

It was the biggest show-stopper of all time for the Murphys.

"Stella, you've hurt me. Screw you and your ultimatum. It's time I told you I've got a son. He's twenty-five now. For a long time I wasn't sure he existed, but he does. We meet for lunch once a week. He looked me up online, and we've been talking for over a year. I love that kid. I'm tired of keeping it secret, fearing your reaction. It's time we come clean. Ernesto knows all about it. He's been a wonderful friend. He understands my pain. You don't!"

"Ernesto may be your friend, but you're the dumbest man alive if you haven't suspected the truth about Ernesto's wife and me, our afternoons of fantastic sex when you're at work? My God that woman kisses me like she means it. She's hungry for me the way you're hungry for potato chips. Do you really think I don't have needs?"

She started to turn the knife, but Faulkner, being a sweet man, told them gently to go home, whoever they are, and not to come back until they were done jerking him around.

He thought of referring the case to a colleague, then told them he'd be glad to see them for some old-fashioned therapy if they were interested. He wouldn't apologize for sending them into the night without offering an appointment.

While walking to the parking lot, he noticed the Murphys were talking to each other quietly in their car, and wondered what they were saying. They were professionals, after all, so he wasn't going to make predictions. Maybe the car bit was part of their act. He looked at his hands and smiled at the larger mystery. By then the wind had stopped and the air was filled with the heavenly scent of jasmine.

A Final Case for Elizabeth Mars

The initials R.F. were scrawled on the tab of an otherwise blank folder, luminous in the hands of Ernst Waverly. A full minute had passed since the doctor lifted it into a streak of light sailing through his blinds in the late afternoon. When he finally lowered it to his desk, his arm moved no faster than the lowering sun. His psychotherapy notes were minimal by intention, but it was unusual for him to write nothing at all, especially about a woman as perplexing as R.F, a self-described mystic, 37, an author of fiction, married, or so she said. He'd seen her for five sessions but had not ventured even one word to record her presence in his life and practice. Only her initials were on the tab, in script, in fine blue ink, from a pen he rarely used.

The details of their encounters swirled inside him, much like the cream in his coffee. The sensation was that of a spiral moment followed by a vanishing. He waited, took a sip, and turned toward the window. The fading light caught him in a frown, the kind he gets in October. Instead of sitting down to write a few sentences or study the scene outside, he fixed his eyes on bits of dust suspended in the air. Of course they were there all along.

When R.F. first came to his office, he offered a hand in introduction, which she touched but didn't grasp. She set her small purse on the couch, turned like a dancer, and sat in the chair near the door as if she simply discovered herself sitting there. It occurred to Waverly she didn't want to declare a need. He had to glean it from the way she leaned—two inches forward so that her back didn't actually touch the chair. The quality of her alertness, the straightness of her posture, the economy of expressions, gave him freedom to sort through his impressions and toss them aside when nothing distilled. *She's building toward something,* he surmised, thinking of the warm-up sounds of the San Francisco Symphony, when musicians come onstage and wander among the chairs to find their places. It was often his favorite part of a concert, a grand cacophony in the tuning of instruments. He would wait, and in the waiting, something amazing would take form.

For once, he had no rush to push or pull. Still, something was odd about the way R.F. said she was married. The sentence didn't reside comfortably with the sentences before and after. The moment felt rehearsed, like she expected him to write it down simply because she said it, or she wanted him to believe it without knowing why it was important. But he didn't move or reach for a pen, and didn't avert his soft blue eyes from the deepening browns of hers. Instead, he followed her through a maze.

It led back to the start. He tried to recall what they actually said in their initial encounter, but the sequence didn't come. He could only remember the world outside, where large yellow leaves from a liquidambar fell without flair, traveling straight down, making minimal turns in the journey. It was so unlike the maple leaves, dancing their waltz of red. Behind them, teardrop leaves from a Bradford pear still clung to their branches, fluttering before surrender. He stood at the sleek glass window, framed by oranges and reds on nearly naked branches, with his fingers at the edge of the folder. All of it played like an adagio.

When thoughts returned they came in densities, like rings in the stump of an ancient redwood tree. The eyes are drawn to the centuries across the sanded finish, but everyone knows that a slow hand across the surface is the best way of knowing the years. He moved his hand across the manila folder as if he could know R.F. this way. It produced a sensation of sand pouring through his fingers. Had someone asked him to close his eyes? No, he closed them on his own, but did not feel alone in the image. The Japanese lamp near her chair lighted their porous intimacy. In the hours after their first meeting, he couldn't think about her as someone outside himself. Now, in the place of floating dust, it came to him that this was her effect on him, also a condition; that they sit with each other unfiltered. She needed to imagine him in the scene outside before venturing to the scene inside. She wanted them to walk among the trees outside, where nothing needed to be explained. If so, she might trust him with a story.

Waverly touched the folder again and the sensation of sand returned. He wanted it to be water. Water is unmistakable, navigable. But she made it be sand. After all, it was her life he was approaching, not a matter of what he wanted. Wasn't it just a week ago that green prevailed outside? If he had met R.F. when everything was green, before the warm days and frosty nights, perhaps there wouldn't be other sensations. *What does it mean,* he whispered to himself, *that I've resisted any assembly of thoughts about her?*

No answer came. Not then, not in nightfall or the morning after. When he approached his desk the following day, he had a thought so obvious he didn't want to give it air. It came as a whisper; *she is so much in me.* No gathering of words, no description of her manner or appearance helped him locate her effects on him. It was oddly the same when she was in his presence.

He could say that she was taller than most, but she adjusted her size with long Spanish vowels. He could say that her left hand was tense when it painted the air with waves, but it seemed a diversion from the way she used her heel to dig a small trench in the carpeted floor. In their last encounter, every time she leaned forward, her necklace swayed in the open air, mesmerizing him in concert with her straight black hair. When she placed her arms in her lap, an Oregon beach appeared, rich with weathered driftwood.

By the fifth session he resolved to consult his mentor about the incredible woman who brought such reveries. He would visit Dr. Elizabeth Mars one last time before she dies. He smiled at the thought, realizing he'd been saying that for the last ten years. She told him long ago that if a story doesn't emerge after a handful of sessions, if it doesn't lean one way or another or begin to write itself, he should look for signs of his own hand in the obscurity. She would say something like that, but would only meet his eyes in the last two words of her sentence. Or she'd remark, just as he was leaving, that a soliloquy from a patient is just around the corner, steeping like tea, waiting to be poured.

The thought of visiting his psychoanalyst friend kicked up a familiar wind in Waverly. She would want details and would look at some object while he spoke: the rim of a cup or the back of her hand. He set himself to tell her how R.F. seemed to speak to the books behind him on his shelf, avoiding the chance of eyes. It was the same way a person might regard you as invisible if you stand in front of a cupboard when they are thinking of what they want inside. Not a disrespect exactly, more a question of position. R.F. sighed when she sensed a rising tide in the sequence of his breaths.

In many such moments she saved him from pointless questions, anticipating them uncannily. Dr. Mars would surely ask for the exact words R.F. had spoken, but would have to settle for the ones he remembered. He told her these:

"Dr. Waverly, I want you to know I wasn't referred to you by anyone. I've never seen a therapist before and have little expectation you can help me. I chose you randomly from the phone book because you're close to where I live."

"Your way of mentioning randomness is a story in itself," Waverly said directly, taking a gentle chance. She was too careful for him to accept he was simply a random choice.

She sank into her chair, not expecting him to pause. *So we didn't choose each other, but here we are,* thought Waverly. He could have actually said it, but didn't.

"Well, your online presence said you treat anxiety, among other things. I don't want to analyze the cause. I don't want to work it through. I'm an author of fiction. Characters don't want to be solved and I don't want you to know me by my history. I want this anxiety to stop bothering me, that's all. It blocks me at every turn."

Waverly sipped his Earl Gray tea. "I'm afraid I can't simply lift it from you. Forgive my persistence, but perhaps it can't be simple, and that may prove to be the deeper satisfaction. I'm hoping we share a belief that character is about development. I respect the road is not straight."

"I will not forgive you anything in advance. You're describing an ancient civilization with layers of mythology. I've already come from these places, survived them, written about them in my stories. I live in their wake. Isn't that enough?"

He answered with lowered eyes. "You live in their wake? Do you believe a new story can rise from the ashes of another?" A pause of the exquisite kind filled the air. He added, "You mentioned surviving," but made sure not to make it a question. He did not chase her, or want to, and left his comment to her care.

R.F. responded by turning her head to find his roses from their scent. They were white, in a cluster of five, close to the Japanese lamp. He saw her profile in brilliant colors, of a woman afraid to leave her home, trying to say something important while concealing herself at the same time. He saw her the way a hummingbird makes a brief stop on a branch before it darts above the trees.

In the flight of images, Waverly almost forgot these were the treasures he would bring to Dr. Mars, the treasures he'd collected in his pocket during a walk in the woods. He chose the moment to phone Dr. Mars at the Sierra Assisted Living Community. She answered on the seventh ring. Even when the phone was within easy reach, she waited at least five rings to assess whether she was in a mood to speak to anyone. At ninety-two, she was full of gravel and wit.

Life in the community was seductive in its comforts, but she found the sea of white-haired residents in the dining room to be more than she bargained for, and countered it by putting an extra dash of motion in her red Irish hair. "Our culture is savage when it comes to aging," she was fond of saying.

"I want a communal solution, a large home on an acre, with five or six friends, a caretaker family, a garden and a big dumb dog." She was delighted to hear Waverly's voice on the phone.

"Please come over tonight," she said. "You will save me from something, I'm sure."

While still on the phone, she took deep breaths in order to ponder the vacancy between his words. She knew he was befuddled since his voice dropped off and he couldn't seem to lift it. He thought it was uncanny, the way she could read him, but she insisted there was nothing uncanny at all. In fact, he was the most transparent man she knew, and she knew quite a few. It amused her to no end to jog him from his seriousness. After thirty years of supervision, they'd become friends and something more, which neither tried to define. Still on the phone, she said, "I have a difficult case of my own, Dr. Waverly. The patient is *me*. I fear my memory is going fast, so please don't miss any traffic lights. I might forget you called." She always made some little joke.

"I'm on my way, twenty minutes," he said, and hung up. His only stop was to buy her a medley of mums. He found her on the second floor down the second hall. She loved the mums, and placed them in a large glass in the kitchen since she couldn't find a vase. He enjoyed seeing her in motion. All these years and she was still a tall vine, expanding in several directions at once, weaving around objects in an artful way. She was halting this time, but upheld tradition, asking him to sit in a chair covered by a blue blanket.

She brought him tea with a heavy shot of brandy. The place she had for him offered a slight imbalance, favoring shadow over light. It was a feature in every drawing she made, and Waverly was always curious about the way she positioned his chair, near a window, angled away from the corner a few inches more than you would think. The effect was to prevent the comfort of symmetry, which she always felt enslaved people. He never asked her about it because questions have a way of ruining everything that is delicate.

In taking his seat, he noticed the smaller things: the book Elizabeth had been reading, the dirty dishes in the sink and the button she missed in the middle of her blouse. Normally, they would exchange a few more pleasantries, but she asked him to jump right in. It caught him off guard and made him revisit the question of whether to describe the person of R.F., or to begin with R.F.'s effects on him. Elizabeth always went for the treasured cashew in the bowl of mixed nuts. She wanted to hear the words he exchanged with his new patient, the images and afterimages, not his assumptions. It sent him to the land of sensations.

Presenting a case to Elizabeth was never easy. Aside from offering a gracious welcome, she did nothing to make it easy, and was not one to give a nod or even a faint smile of encouragement when he was talking. She simply accepted what he said; that he was flooded with images when meeting R.F. and he wondered if these represented a bridge he was missing or an alternate language of some kind. What would it mean if her stories were a smoke-screen? He told Elizabeth about the blank folder and the fact he remembered the trees outside more than the actual exchange of words. He made a point of asking if it could be natural that images are the heart of an intimate exchange, not the chosen words. He didn't expect answers.

Talking out loud changed everything. The shadow from the lampshade made an arc on Elizabeth's blouse. Night was coming on and it changed the mood of the wind. Backgrounds were changing too, like a kaleidoscope, but he couldn't be sure who was turning the cylinder. Something was different about Elizabeth. When he described how R.F. looked past him to his books, he noticed Elizabeth's books were in disarray.

Then, for no reason he understood, he told of a dream he had about R.F., where the image of an egg timer appeared between them in the middle of a session. In the dream they did not speak about it or think it was unusual. They were speaking, but words didn't make the journey to each other.

Elizabeth perked up like any good psychoanalyst does when a dream is mentioned as part of a casual association. "So in the dream you both saw it! How do you think your patient might have experienced the egg timer? Pretend you're still in the dream. Say what comes to mind."

"I'll try," said Waverly, "but it will only be my fantasy." Elizabeth rolled her eyes as if he'd just announced that a piece of wood is a piece of wood. He ventured that R.F. would have described herself as the sand on top. Grain by grain, obedient to gravity, she would fill his portion of the joined glass, giving him all her stories. But in that version, knowing R.F., he was keenly aware she would eventually feel depleted. Then it came to him that her ability to tolerate her own depletion was the gift she might value the most—the moment when he could actually help her see that she was vibrant and very much alive.

Then he turned it around. If he was the sand on top, and she the empty half, he didn't want to fill her space with only his *ideas* about her, which can easily happen when therapists are too much in love with their theories. It was one of his eternal discussions with Elizabeth Mars.

Elizabeth watched him struggle, taking it all in before commenting. Nothing moved, nothing descended. Finally, she spoke.

"It's a bad analogy, a worse metaphor, and a terrible way to think about what happens between people. But this is the most honest dream I've heard in a long time, a fabulous condensation I believe Freud might say. I prefer the way Philip Bromberg thinks. After all, you didn't think the dream into existence. It came upon your canvas.

"So here I am," he said to Elizabeth, "stuck with all these different thoughts. For the first time in a long while, I wanted to share my own dream with a patient. I didn't since I don't want to impose anything. I often wonder why I hold back, whether I should just take a chance and let my patients know I have an inner world of my own. Once in a careful moment, that is. I'm in the mist with her, and I admit part of me wants to stay there. Here's a fantasy resolution: either R.F. or I will turn the egg timer over, or rest it on its side, and each of us will be partially filled by the stream of the other's presence. Either way, it seems we must try to comment on the thing between us, to find a way to talk about it."

"Why do you need a resolution? You do not need my interpretation here. You need another brandy," she said, "and so do I."

He caught himself noticing a tremor in Elizabeth's hand when she poured them fresh drinks, but her eyes told him not to say anything. He kept on about the dream, the sand, the passage of time, telling her he'd stumbled into a conundrum because stopping the egg timer would cause the end of motion, and motion is what makes people real to each other. He placed an ice cube in his mouth and continued, talking around the cube.

"You know, what I really want is for both of us to break the egg timer so it spills in a beautiful mess. Why can't we be on a ship or a train, able to go from one end to the other, to appreciate what's coming and going with freedom of movement? Why can't I have that dream instead?" Only the houseplants answered, with their stubborn green tones. He ambled through the thickets, not looking at Elizabeth, trusting she would eventually invite him to say more. And she did.

"You said your patient writes fiction. I think you'll have a conversation about that soon, and you'll see if you can set aside what you imagine. You'll see if you can hear what she actually says. There will be a gap, maybe the Grand Canyon, but it will be absolutely essential to avoid getting in the way. The conversations will exist in parallels at first, at least that's what always happened with me when I worked with artists. You won't be able to resist the draw when she tells you about her work in her own way, only when she's ready. For now, you must merely set the stage. And for God's sake don't start out by asking her what her current story is all about. If you do, you'll miss the plot within the plot."

"I'm a little guilty on that, but only a little, since she started talking about it in her last session, and possibly I'd been giving hints that weren't too subtle—as to my curiosity. All these years and I'm still a novice. It was good that she initiated, and that I tried to make room for anything, since she feared I would be an intruder. I wonder about these things, how the unsaid is expressed anyway. When she started, it was so riveting it felt like a crime to end the session, but it was the beginning of the next chapter."

Elizabeth looked out the window like she was looking back in time. Her eyes narrowed, then closed, leaving Waverly with the impression she was bringing herself to the dream to see the scene for herself. Her hair was like a storm, her brow a map of rivers.

He looked around the room and noticed a pile of mail had been stuffed under the couch. It was very unlike her and he began to worry. He also wondered if she'd simply fallen asleep.

In less than a minute she returned, like she never went away. "Speaking of time, I must take my medication now, please excuse me." She got up, found a pill, and chased it with a shot of brandy. Normally she had just one brandy, and never drank it quickly.

"Back to your case," she insisted, "it's always a problem forcing meaning into things. But it's always revealing about the one who needs the meaning, and nobody can easily stop whatever it is they're doing. Not for long that is. We may simply be in the business of making more room, smashing walls to make more room. Don't you think that's all we do sometimes?" She did not expect an answer, and followed her thought by touching the side of her face the way her mother might have done in the first hour of her life.

"Let's say your egg timer represents the tyranny of time, so of course you want to break it. In your fantasy, both you and R.F. want to break the egg timer. Count me in on the wish. We live in these fifty-minute snippets of time, and sometimes we hate it, but our patients hate it more. We should be amazed by what gets accomplished in spite of it."

She moved her hand to her knee and made an angry fist.

"Never forget that time will chase you and crush you in the end. It will take your sand castle back to sea and leave the beach pristine. You have this fantastic new patient and I wish you all the time and presence you need. It's odd. Now that I'm thinking about dying, the early years of my practice are some of my clearest memories. They come when they will. I used to doubt it, now I see them like crystals in morning dew."

Waverly felt something in his spine. He started to ask about her memories, but she went under again, to a land of frozen tundra, and returned with an icy face that was slow to become reacquainted with the Elizabeth he knew. He saw her briefly as a sleeping child, a college student, a wild woman dancing solo in Golden Gate Park, stoned and free to roam. He took a sip of brandy. You can know something but need reminding; Elizabeth was ninety-two.

She did not look well. He fought the thought. No, she was still herself, cleverly catching nuances, maybe a little tired. Couldn't they just be travelling down a familiar street with him by her side, offering his arm while she offered her brilliant ideas. How easily he remembered her thirty years ago with those same flaring eyes. She spoke of things that mattered.

"Ernst, when you are most confused, there's your open door. I'm not talking about blind spots. People live perfectly decent lives when they're broken up in pieces. I used to place too much emphasis in how the pieces are connected. But I know you precisely because you are like me. You won't rest until there's a connection, will you?"

"I suppose not," he said, "maybe there's no cure for us."

"On that we fully agree. Then we must look for a passage, not a cure," she quipped.

He also remembered her major stroke many years before, when she had to leave her artisan home and office. He helped her move the boxes, all her files, her poetry and drawings. Childless by choice, it was hard for her at the facility when residents bragged endlessly about grandchildren. She had a devious side.

"Dr. Waverly, would you think lesser of me if I simply invent a superstar grandchild to keep up? Who would challenge it? Children have imaginary friends, why can't I have an imaginary grandchild?" He told her it seemed like a grand idea, but to reserve it for just the right moment, for just the right braggart, a trump card for when she really needed one. With her imagination, it would be a doozy.

Elizabeth also complained about the Northern Wall, as she called it, after dinner, where residents tended to congregate to share medical complaints and mean-spirited opinions of other residents in the room; people who were nearly deaf, or struggled with a spoon. Dark energy fascinated her. She couldn't believe the hostility. Last week she ventured near their circle and asked a rhetorical question like she was genuinely confused.

"Why do we find it so easy to be mean when we could just as easily be kind?" If someone wanted to engage her, she regarded it as a victory over the Northern Wall, and the bonus was considerable in that she made a new friend for brandy.

Waverly tried to go the heart of it a while back. "It must be terribly sad to be the healthiest one among your ailing friends." Her closest friend down the hall had become a prisoner in her body. All they could share was the sweetness of voice and touch. It was only a month ago that another friend just didn't wake up one morning.

"Yes, yes, it's all true," she said, "If I have another stroke, I hope it's all she wrote."

A rogue wave disrupted Waverly's memories. Elizabeth opened her eyes and resumed.

"We had an egg timer in my family. It was my mother's. She said I was too impatient, and she used the timer to demand my silence after the smallest misbehavior. I took to hiding it and one day I broke it, just snapped the thing in two. I buried it under a cedar sapling and lied about it. That tree is probably eighty feet tall by now. You're the only one who knows. I want you to know it's still there. Consider it my inheritance, a private response to a silencing voice. But that was another world, now lets get back to your case."

Suddenly, Elizabeth began speaking in a mock British accent. "You have such compelling diversions, Dr. Waverly, but don't forget how cunning I am. You were saying something about a dream." Now she was a little drunk, a little unfolded.

Waverly said yes, indeed he was, but needed to excuse himself to use the bathroom. On the way back, he got himself another shot of brandy, absent the tea. She flipped her hand in permission, and rested her eyes once more. From his perch in the kitchen, he noticed a prescription on the counter. He didn't want to snoop, but that's how people are, and he saw it was for Aricept, which he knew was prescribed for mild cognitive impairment, often in the early stages of dementia.

A trail of broken crackers led to a poem on the counter, handwritten in pencil, shaky but bold. She could easily have hidden the Aricept, also the poem, but didn't. Waverly sighed like the mountains and set himself to the sum of his observations: deterioration in her handwriting, a grocery list with misspellings, forks in the place where she kept her spatulas. The floor was sticky too. It gathered in him as sadness, then guilt, for he'd been selfish in thinking she would always be there for him in the usual ways. Ah, but she was still sharp and must have had a shock at the doctor. Still, the falling leaves and willing earth did not prepare him for her poem. With one hand on the counter, the other holding his drink, he read what she had written.

My Great and Final Wish

Release me to the wolves
So I might run among them
Heavy in our winter coats
Where breath is hot

And the hunt is on.
Release me from a body
That withers, unable to run.
I have no more words

For what I've become
And would chase a chance
To leave this form, chase it
Through a sharp tangle

Of blackberries, past the lake
And beyond. I hear a call
So clear and pure I'll find
The trail in soft white snow.

Elizabeth Mars, M.D.

Next to the poem was a pamphlet about dementia, the symptoms, the reminders of uneven progression. No two paths are the same. What it didn't mention was the undoing of life's constructions. She knew it all from being a doctor, but not from the patient's chair. Waverly walked to his place by the window and it brought her back to speech.

"Tell me, Dr. Waverly, has your patient told you what was going on when she had her first panic attack?"

"Elizabeth, I have to tell you I've read your poem, I saw the prescription. Please tell me what's going on. I want to help any way I can." She gathered herself and admitted she wasn't joking over the phone when she said her memory was failing. It was serious, all too real. Even her doctor dreaded giving her condition the name she feared for years.

"Thank you, my excellent friend. Names and faces are starting to elude me, but not yours. Not yet. The best way to help me will be to tell me about your patient. I'm still me. Do not skip a beat, or I shall get cross."

"How can I talk about a patient when you are facing such trouble?"

"Because I'll pummel you with my cane if you back away from me in pity!"

A path appeared, a respect, and something more.

"All right, I'll try. Give me a moment."

In his pause he thought of the night before, when the crescent moon was just a sliver, but it allowed him to see the whole sphere against the sky. It felt unreal, the cycle of earth's shadow, the seasons of life, and he remembered Elizabeth had outlived two husbands. The first was an architect, the second an engineer. She wore their gifts, a bracelet and a necklace, to keep them close. Friends knew she had a tattoo of a rose on her hip, but she never described its origins. She saw him looking at her jewelry, and she brushed him off with a glance. "In one life there are many," she once said, "I came of age in the '60s. Now, please, continue."

"Well," Waverly said, reluctantly, "R.F. was reluctant to give any kind a synopsis of her fictional story. Finally she felt the need. She was writing her first science fiction story about a young woman living on a space transport ship on the way to exploring the interior of Hyperion, one of the sixty-two moons of Saturn. The moon has the appearance of a sponge, with an irregular orbit. She was experimenting, free-associating we might say, to give her main character a history, a personality, making her a compelling protagonist. She wrote her character as a scientist who had to constantly defend her choices, since she was responsible for choosing which moon might have the most rare metals deep beneath the surface. Even in her futuristic vision, it requires extra courage to be a woman who wants to be a geologist in space exploration. To add complexity, the character finds out in the middle of her journey into space she'd been adopted in her first year of life."

Elizabeth took a sip of brandy and smiled at the ice cubes in her glass. "Don't stop there," she admonished, pulling her blanket over her shoulders as if she was camping in the woods.

"She discovers it all by accident looking at her personnel file while updating material for her resume. She finds adoption papers showing her birth mother gave her up, and she doesn't know why. The file used to be restricted, but she's become an expert at finding things she's not supposed to know. Now she has to find out why. It shakes her world, her confidence as she's hurtling through space."

"You're torturing me, Dr. Waverly. Why do you pause so long?"

"R.F. told me all this, but she couldn't believe her story had any relevance to her as the author. She thought it was just a fancy. I pushed a bit, only a bit, and she finally said she didn't know why she wrote it, or where the ideas even came from. She thought it was a random mix of parts from novels, T.V. or movies. After all, she was looking for an arc for her story, and she thought this one fell from the sky. All she remembers is her heart pounding, the walls closing in, and six hours later she woke in the corner of her room in a fetal position."

He told Elizabeth how E.F.'s panic attacks were becoming more frequent, triggered by the slightest mother-daughter theme.

"She stopped writing altogether, stopped going out of the house. She was separated from her husband. It didn't occur to her to call him, and she told me it felt as though they were never actually married. She felt that the relationship was rather solid until she realized she couldn't go to him with any real problems. He's a decent guy; it's just that she describes him as a stranger. After her first panic attacks, she tried yoga, mystical exercises, centering mantras, and yet she swears she found me randomly. Now that we're together, she puts a meaning to it, a kind of magic I don't believe in, but here it is; a mist I've never felt before. I find myself wanting to be with her more. It's a strange seduction, the urge for a next session."

Elizabeth became intensely alert listening to Waverly, as if the story was the juice of life and her own problems belonged to someone down the hall.

"Yes, go on," she said, "you know I'm a sucker for a story that's unfolding. I honestly can't help myself. There's no cure for me either. I hope you're not making R.F. up just to keep me going."

"Well, I'm getting to the confusing part, but first I want to say that R.F. seemed reassured that I was offering something of value in talking about her fiction, when at first she made it clear it was forbidden territory. I listened and tried to ground her in the safety of my office, the familiar objects there, and of course, my voice. At the same time, she won't let me talk *about* it, only to hear it. She still doesn't think there's any link between her story and the panic attacks, the protagonist finding out she was adopted, the transport ship to the moon of Saturn, the unreal husband, the fetal position.

"Yes, and the confusing part for you?"

"Well, it's coming to me now. At the end of our last session, when she got up to leave, she couldn't get her coat on. She wasn't wearing it when she came in from the waiting room. It didn't feel like she was acting, not like a histrionic display of helplessness or a cue for me to play a part. I think I'd sense that. I would simply help her in an awkward moment, but the moment wasn't simple. As I saw her struggle to put on the coat, I also saw it was much too small for her, a child's coat, and there was no way she could get it on. When she saw what I saw, she recoiled and frowned, and left the room with the coat dangling off of her arm. She didn't mention it the next time I saw her, and I chose to leave it alone and see if she would allude to it later, or whether it was truly a dissociated moment."

Elizabeth was famous for creating an image of a person she would never meet. She had a gift as a clinician, a quality that helped her chase her ideas around corners, to streets with other thoughts.

"So, you're saying she came with a coat that didn't fit and it turned out to be a child's coat. And you're right to assume her unconscious was at work. She needed you to see it, but the need couldn't be known to her. It's good that you didn't force her to see what you saw just then. Your patient didn't have children of her own, so it must have been her own coat from long ago. It's going to be a key part of your work together, but you won't be able to access this for quite a while. I hate this dementia. I won't remember what I just said in a few weeks. I'll be talking about the stain on the carpet, how it got there. People will remind me I spilled coffee there two months ago. They'll remind me I'm a psychoanalyst, and I'll say I'd like a cookie now. Can't we just break the egg timer together?"

"I'm so sorry. You are such a bright light to me, Elizabeth."

"Well, this light is growing dim. Now shut up and let me think. There was a time when the coat must have fit R.F. perfectly, when it protected her and was important.

Otherwise she wouldn't have tried to put it on in front of you. Something has derailed her. I've always wondered about writers of fiction, how much it feels like memoir in disguise. You've got big-time dissociation here, and you're trying to respect what is being acted out. My God how I envy you the chance to help her, however long it takes."

From her soft brown chair, Elizabeth peered out the window of her assisted-living flat, looking at nothing in particular.

"Let me tell you about one of my first patients. She comes to me now. Her name was Ernesta. It was about forty years ago. Her husband had been murdered and she came to me in abject grief, needing to find, among the shattered places, a reason not to kill herself and the baby she was carrying. I was so green, I resorted to begging her to think beyond the abyss, beyond the silence of her rooms, to the life inside her. I stayed with her through the anger, the absence of reason, so many empty hours, a few involuntary hospitalizations. We came to know each other in the oddest ways, the ways the eyes have always known. She knew I was helpless when I tried to sip tea out of my empty cup. I knew she was bereft when she smiled as if she was fine. I even burdened her with an apology that I couldn't do more than I did. She finally resolved to have the child, and brought her beautiful daughter to a session to meet me. Her name was Rosalinda."

Waverly was transfixed with the lucidity of Elizabeth's story. It was rare for him to hear about her early work, her mix of helplessness and raw determination. He had trouble imagining her as anything but confident. He tried for an overview.

"The uncomplicated parts of caring are best, kindness and persistence."

"But it wasn't enough," Elizabeth said, "because a short time later Ernesta gave up Rosalinda for adoption and disappeared from treatment. I tried to intervene, but there was no other relative, no avenue, no respite care back then, and the treatments for post-partum depression were minimal. It's been a burden not to know what happened to Rosalinda and her mother. I count it among my sorrows. Tell me, Dr. Waverly, what stands out the most as you speak of your dear R.F.?"

Waverly hesitated, losing himself in Ernesta's lonely decision. The great kaleidoscope turned to an all-blue world.

"Elizabeth, I swear I don't know what to make of this, but my patient's first name is Rosalinda, and she found out her birth mother was named Ernesta. What are the chances?"

He lifted from his chair, held a hand to his brow, and turned fully around in the place he stood. Elizabeth missed a breath and only resumed when he rested his hand on her shoulder. They were statues then, humbled in discovery. Night was upon them in earnest and a faint smile crossed the lips of Elizabeth Mars.

"What are the chances Rosalinda has come to me this way? It's like she's put me to bed with a kiss on my forehead."

She wept the way a mother does when a child returns from war.

"I don't pretend to know. We don't get to know very much about what happens to people do we?" He picked up his glass and finished it. Elizabeth asked him to fill hers with ice and a splash of water. He ventured past her poem on the kitchen counter, thinking of circles and bits of dust.

She labored to keep her eyes open to receive the glass. It was not a time to talk. Their glasses met, slightly off-center of course, in a toast of sorts, never to be voiced. When she drifted off, Waverly found her favorite blanket that had fallen to the floor during the evening. He covered her frail shoulders in the soft warm cotton and dimmed the lights while she slept. Time was not invited. He swirled the naked cubes in his glass, around and around and around, until they finally turned to water

About the Author

J.L. COOPER is an author and psychologist in Sacramento, California. His writing highlights the lyricism in everyday life, relational mysteries, and the elevation of subjective experience. He has received five literary awards in fiction, nonfiction, poetry, and essay, including the *Tupelo Quarterly Prose Open Prize*, TQ9, judged by Pulitzer winner Adam Johnson, and the Grand Prize in Poetry, *Crosswinds Poetry Journal*, 2018, judged by Pulitzer winner in criticism Lloyd Schwartz. His full-length book of poetry, *An Ocean Large Enough* (David Robert Books) is available on Amazon Books. His short stories, poetry and a craft piece have appeared or are forthcoming in numerous journals including *The Manhattan Review*, *The Comstock Review*, *New Millennium Writings*, *Oberon Poetry Magazine*, *StoryQuarterly*, *Cutthroat*, *Hippocampus*, *Leveler*, *The Tishman Review*, *3Elements Review*, *Structo*, and several other journals and anthologies. His website is: jlcooper.net.

Also by J.L. Cooper

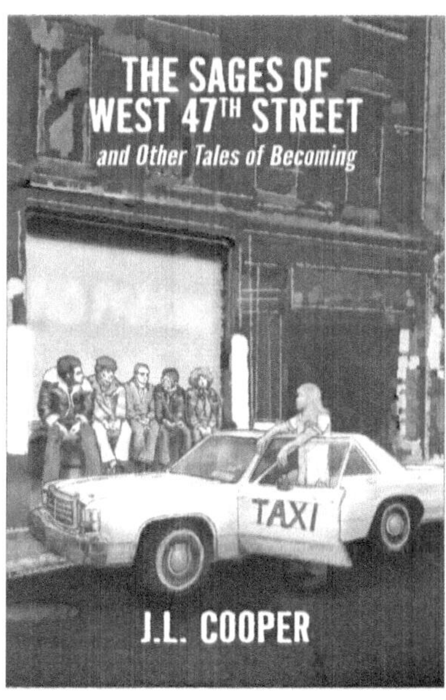

Available through Amazon, Barnes & Noble,
Book Depository, and most online book retailers.

Forthcoming from J.L. Cooper

Driving at Night in October
A poetry chapbook

Spell of the Pelicans
A novella

PO Box #3092
Citrus Heights, CA 95611-3092
fivewarblers.wordpress.com